For more than forty years,
Yearling has been the leading name
in classic and award-winning literature
for young readers.

Yearling books feature children's
favorite authors and characters,
providing dynamic stories of adventure,
humor, history, mystery, and fantasy.

Trust Yearling paperbacks to entertain,
inspire, and promote the love of reading
in all children.

This is a work of fiction. Names, characters, places, and incidents either are the product of the author's imagination or are used fictitiously. Any resemblance to actual persons, living or dead, events, or locales is entirely coincidental.

Copyright © 1994 by Gary Paulsen
Map copyright © 1994 by Virginia Norey

All rights reserved. Published in the United States by Yearling, an imprint of Random House Children's Books, a division of Random House, Inc., New York. Originally published in hardcover in the United States by Delacorte Press, an imprint of Random House Children's Books, a division of Random House, Inc., New York, in 1994.

Yearling and the jumping horse design are registered trademarks of Random House, Inc.

Visit us on the Web! www.randomhouse.com/kids

Educators and librarians, for a variety of teaching tools, visit us at
www.randomhouse.com/teachers

Library of Congress Cataloging-in-Publication Data is available upon request.

ISBN 978-0-440-41133-8 (pbk.)

Printed in the United States of America

41 40 39 38 37 36 35 34 33 32

Random House Children's Books supports the First Amendment
and celebrates the right to read.

MR. TUCKET

★

GARY PAULSEN

A YEARLING BOOK

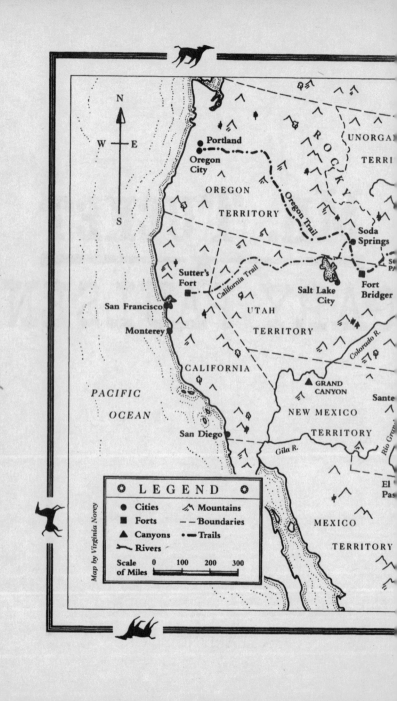

N
W   E
S

Portland
Oregon City

OREGON
TERRITORY

ROCKY

UNORGAN
TERRI

Oregon Trail

Soda
Springs

S
PA

Sutter's
Fort

California Trail

Salt Lake
City

Fort
Bridger

San Francisco

Monterey

UTAH

TERRITORY

Colorado R.

CALIFORNIA

PACIFIC

OCEAN

San Diego

GRAND
CANYON

NEW MEXICO

TERRITORY

Gila R.

Sante

Rio Grande

El
Pas

LEGEND

● Cities
■ Forts
▲ Canyons
≈ Rivers

⌃⌃ Mountains
– – Boundaries
•– Trails

MEXICO

TERRITORY

Scale
of Miles

0   100   200   300

Map by Virginia Norey

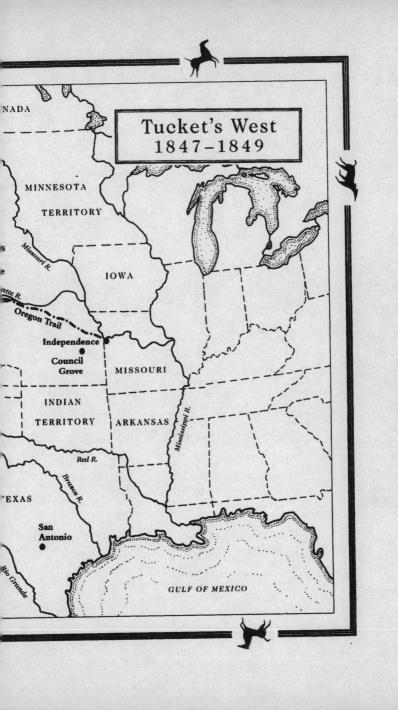

Tucket's West
1847–1849

NADA

MINNESOTA
TERRITORY

IOWA

Missouri R.

Platte R.

Oregon Trail

Independence

Council
Grove

MISSOURI

INDIAN

TERRITORY ARKANSAS

Mississippi R.

Red R.

Brazos R.

EXAS

San
Antonio

Rio Grande

GULF OF MEXICO

Chapter One

FRANCIS ALPHONSE TUCKET came back to life slowly. He didn't open his eyes. He didn't want to open his eyes until he remembered everything that had happened.

Yesterday had been Francis's fourteenth birthday, and he had celebrated it quietly. Usually his mother and father—and even his nine-year-old sister Rebecca—made a big thing of birthdays. They had friends in, and a giant cake cooked to perfection on his mother's huge wood-burning stove, and by four in the afternoon everybody was so full of homemade ice cream and cake they couldn't move.

But that was how it had been on the farm in Missouri, where they had had the big house and barn. Yesterday they had celebrated Francis's birthday on the tailgate of a Conestoga wagon at the foothills of the Rocky Mountains. It was June 13, 1847—a warm summer Tuesday in a new country and they were with a wagon train on its way to Oregon. Francis, on awakening that morning, thought that even without any sort of birthday party, it would be his best birthday yet. How many boys of fourteen had ever seen drawings of the Rockies, let alone the real thing? That was an adventure in itself, not to mention crossing the great Kansas plains and watching the train scout, Mr. Ballard, hunt buffalo for the wagon train.

But then there had been a party—or at least a sort of party. As the wagons had squared away for the day's journey westward, Francis's mother called him from helping his father hitch some oxen to the yoke and tongue of the wagon. He went to the rear, where she was, and there, sitting on the tailgate, was a cake. He had no idea how she had done it—her stove was way back in Missouri, too heavy for the wagon. And he had not seen her doing anything special on the buffalo-chip fire that morning—but there it was, a cake. And easily one of the nicest cakes he'd ever seen.

"Happy fourteenth birthday, Alphonse," she said, with a smile. She had always called him Alphonse. His father always called him Francis.

For a long moment he didn't answer, just stood staring at the cake. Then he thanked her, knowing it would do no good to ask her how she'd done it. She would just answer, "Where there's a will, there's a way," as she always explained things that seemed impossible to Francis.

"Would you like a piece now?" she asked. "Or would you rather wait until tonight? The train is going to stop early today. Mr. Ballard wants to check all the wagons before we get to the mountains."

He wanted a piece so badly his mouth was watering, but he knew that wasn't what she expected, so he hid his eagerness. "We could have a sort of party," he suggested. "I could ask Ike and Max over and maybe offer them some cake." Ike and Max were the only other two boys in the train. There were five girls, but they kind of kept to themselves after Max threw a garter snake on one of them.

"That's a good idea," his mother said, nodding. "I'll wrap it in muslin and save it for this evening."

He could tell that he had pleased her. In all

truth, he didn't really want to share the cake with Ike and Max. Oh, they were nice enough, but they weren't really friends. It just happened that they were the only other boys, and Francis was more or less forced to do things with them. Ike would have been all right except that he talked funny and did things in an odd way. He said "thee" and "thou" and his folks always made him wear black clothes and a black flat-brimmed hat. Francis's father had said they were Quakers from the East somewhere, and that they all talked like that, but Francis still found it hard to get used to somebody calling him "friend" all the time.

Max was an out-and-out bully, and Francis wouldn't talk to him at all under normal conditions. But in the wagon train he had to. Max kept finding him when the wagons stopped for the night, and it was either talk or fight. They had fought several times, before Francis had found it easier to talk.

And in fighting they were pretty evenly matched. Their worst fight had taken place the time Max had teased Ike—short for Ichabod. Ike wouldn't fight, no matter how many bad names Max called him. Finally Max had hit Ike on the shoulder. That had made Francis mad and he'd torn into Max and given him a bloody nose, which got him a licking from his father that night, but he didn't care. The licking hadn't been much—he knew his father was doing it because there was no other way to keep Max's mother from complaining all over the train—and his father hadn't used a switch the way he did when Francis did something really bad. He had used his hand, and had smacked only twice, lightly, hiding a grin.

So Francis wasn't all that eager to share his cake with Ike and Max, but it pleased his mother—and he hadn't expected a cake anyway.

The idea of getting a present wasn't even on his mind that Tuesday morning. The nearest store was over five hundred miles away and he knew, or thought he knew, every item in the wagon. He'd helped load it, and there hadn't been any presents, or anything that had looked like presents. But they'd fooled him again. When he got back to the front of the wagon, to help his father finish with the oxen, he was handed a long, thin bundle wrapped in butcher's paper.

"Happy birthday, Francis," his father said, smiling. "We figured that it was about time you had one of these."

Francis was really puzzled, until his fingers tore away some of the paper. He didn't need to unwrap it all to know what it was. Already the sun hit a brass fitting, some dark, hand-rubbed walnut, and the brown sheen of polished steel.

"A rifle." His voice was soft. "A *new* rifle. But how . . . I mean, I helped load the wagon, and I didn't see it."

"The Petersons carried it in their wagon for me," his father said. "I brought it over to ours last night while you were sleeping. Do you like it?"

By this time Francis had torn off the rest of the paper and was finding it hard to keep from bouncing in excitement.

"It's a Lancaster," his father explained. "I think probably the only one of its kind. I thought about buying you a Hawkens in St. Louis, but they only make heavy rifles that fire heavy balls. When I talked to Mr. Lancaster, he said that a smaller caliber was more accurate, and with just a bit more powder, gave as much power as a big ball. Oh, the bullet mold, percussion caps, and powder flask are still in Mr. Peterson's wagon."

Francis could do nothing but stare at the rifle. Its stock, going only halfway up the barrel and bound to the metal with hand-forged brass bands, was of burled walnut. The lock, hammer, and trigger had been case-hardened in new oil, so they looked like etched marble instead of steel, and the barrel was the deepest, richest brown he had ever seen. The whole weapon had been made smaller than a full-sized rifle—just right for a fourteen-year-old boy. Even the sights, full elk-horn design for easy sighting, seemed to be in miniature.

"You mean . . ." Francis hesitated. There was really no way he could express enough thanks. "Did you really have this made just for me?"

"Then you do like it," his father said, smiling again. "I was worried about that. I thought maybe you wouldn't think too much of owning a rifle." His eyes crinkled. "I'm sure there must be a couple of thousand things a boy would rather own than a rifle—"

"I don't know about other boys," Francis interrupted. "But there isn't even one thing *I'd* want before a rifle. I've been wanting a rifle of my own ever since Mr. Ballard took me out and taught me how to shoot his buffalo gun."

They laughed, both of them remembering how the first shot Francis had taken with the scout's big .60-caliber gun had knocked him back on his rear.

"Well, you don't have to worry about getting knocked over with this one," his father assured Francis. "This is only a .40 caliber. Mr. Lancaster said it was fast, but wouldn't kick too much. The only way to find out is to shoot it, I guess. Why don't you go over to the Petersons' wagon and get the mold, caps, and powder? There's also a bag of lead balls already molded. Then when we pull out, you can drop back of the last wagon and practice shooting buffalo chips."

"Alone?" Francis asked.

"I don't see why not. You know how to handle a weapon—I watched you the other day with Mr. Ballard. Just make sure you don't shoot toward the train. It wouldn't do to break somebody's prize punch bowl."

Francis grinned. The only one in the wagon train foolish enough to carry a punch bowl had been Max's mother—and she bragged about it every chance she got. No, it wouldn't do to break it— especially if *he* did it.

"I'll be careful," Francis said, and started for the Petersons' wagon.

"And make sure you don't stray out of sight," his father called. "Mr. Ballard says there've been some Pawnee in this area. They might like to get their hands on that little rifle of yours."

This time they both smiled. The idea of Indians being around was pretty funny. All across the Kansas plains there had been talk of Indian trouble, and everybody worried about the Comanches. And they hadn't, not once in the whole trip, even seen a feather—let alone an Indian. Francis was almost disappointed. He had looked forward to seeing Indians nearly as much as seeing the mountains.

Francis dropped back from the rear of the train, and failed to notice that he was falling too far back. His forgetfulness was caused by the little rifle. Shooting it was a dream. He couldn't seem to miss, and it didn't kick at all. He got so engrossed in firing it that he didn't see the last wagon pull far ahead.

He lay still now, and tried to remember exactly what happened. He had fired about ten times, he knew, liking the little rifle more each time. On the eleventh or so shot, as he was loading, a large brown hand had clamped itself over his mouth.

His rifle had been grabbed first. There had been seven Indians—six young men and an older warrior. Probably a hunting party, because they hadn't been wearing paint. Then Francis made his first mistake; instead of just relaxing and biding his time until he could get a chance to escape, he fought them. Kicking and swinging and biting, more out of fear than courage, he had given the seven Pawnees a rough few minutes. Finally they'd hit him, just a little tap in back of his ear with his own rifle butt, and he had fallen like a stone.

They had ridden all that day, with Francis draped head-down across the old man's lap, bouncing like a sack of meal. He had passed into and out of consciousness on the trip, and had no idea where they finally dropped him—except that it was a dark and smelly place.

Now it was time to open his eyes. He opened them—then shut them as fast as he could.

Sitting above him, giving him a toothless grin, was the ugliest old person he'd ever seen—he couldn't tell at first if it was a man or a woman. Just a wrinkled face and toothless mouth that smiled when Francis's eyes came open.

Chapter Two

FRANCIS'S CAMP LIFE with the Pawnees began that very morning. The old woman—as it turned out—was the wife of the old man who had been with the hunting party. She tied a rope around his neck and dragged him around the camp like a new puppy. At each lodge she would stop and call the whole family out. Then she would point at Francis and gabble something he couldn't understand. He guessed that she was bragging about her new "son." But he didn't much like what followed. The women would pinch his arms and push his lips back to look at his teeth, while the children—if there were any at the lodge—came out and kicked him.

Francis didn't stand for it at first. When another boy his age kicked him, he kicked right back, and landed a fairly good blow. This made all the adults laugh, but his "mother" shook her head and pulled his neck rope so tight it nearly strangled him. He figured finally that it was easier to play along and let them kick him. For the present it was enough just to stay alive and learn as much as possible about the Pawnees. He might need the information later to escape. And he would escape; he was sure of it. Either alone, or with somebody from the train—probably Mr. Ballard—who would come to rescue him.

In the meantime, he might as well make it as easy as possible on himself. To this end, he smiled at his new "mother."

That was his second mistake. Immediately she returned the smile and took the rope off his neck. That much he liked. But before he could get accustomed to the freedom of movement, three young Indian boys jumped him, and he had to fight like a demon just to stay on his feet. It would have been pretty fair if just one of the young Indians had tackled him. But with three of them climbing all over him Francis had no choice but to fight back any way he could—which meant hitting, biting, and kicking.

What surprised and angered him most was that none of the elders—not even his "mother"—made any move to stop the fight. Instead they just gathered around and cheered. None of them, it seemed, was on Francis's side, and this didn't help him keep his temper. Neither did the fact that he knew he couldn't win against the three boys. After the first five minutes, he decided that if he was going to lose anyway, he might as well do as much damage as possible on the way down. He picked the largest of the Indian boys and went after him. The other two might as well not have been there. One jumped on his back and another grabbed at his legs, but it was all too late to save the boy Francis had concentrated on—he was underneath Francis when the other two forced him down. And for every blow the two boys should have landed, Francis gave the Indian boy under him one on the nose. Even if they killed him for it, he was going to make that boy sorry he'd ever picked a fight.

"Hoka-ha!"

Francis didn't hear the yell, but the two boys on top of him jumped away. Francis just kept hammering away at the boy beneath him, who had now curled into a ball and covered his head with his arms.

"Hoka-ha," came the gruff voice a second time.

"It is enough! You fight with fists—the way a girl fights."

Francis felt himself lifted roughly by the back of his belt and dropped in the dirt. Immediately he swung around and attacked the man who had lifted him. He was struck such a blow that it knocked him head over heels.

"It is *enough*! I will not say it again."

Francis wiped his eyes with the back of his hand. He had expected to see a tall, or at least a strong-looking man. Instead he found himself looking at a short, wiry Indian with his hair in one braid. At the bottom of the braid there was one feather, hanging straight down. The man wore plain buckskins, un-beaded moccasins, and carried a rifle in his left hand. It was Francis's rifle.

"Enough my foot," he said, glaring up at the Indian. "They started it, not me. You want to start knocking somebody around, why not give *them* a lick or two? And if you're so tough, why do you have to steal rifles from boys?"

In a sudden hush of the people gathered around the fighting area, Francis watched in horror as the Indian raised the muzzle of the rifle until it pointed dead between his eyes.

"Bravery in youth is a good thing," the Indian said. He wasn't smiling. "It is not good to be stupid, little white-eyed wolf. It is stupid to insult the man who holds your gun. It is stupid to insult your elders. If you do it again, I will kill you."

The Indian let the rifle down easily and spun away. Francis watched him go, kneeling there in the dirt. He had never seen such a pure, cold look in a man's eyes, and he knew that he would have to be very careful whenever the one-braided warrior was around.

— Chapter Three —

THREE WEEKS AFTER he came to the Pawnee camp, Francis learned that the brave who had threatened to kill him, and had purchased the rifle for two good horses from the old man who had led the party, was named Braid. Braid was a war leader. He was not a chief, but any time there was a need for a raid, Braid was the man who led the war party. In camp he was just another warrior, except that he was so mean that many people feared him. He had the scalps of many "victories" braided around the doorway to his lodge. He did not dress in finery, the way many warriors did, because he didn't need to impress anybody. His scalps did that for him.

Francis hated Braid more than anything on earth. He watched him lead out a big party of more than forty warriors. They were gone all that day and through the night until the next morning.

When they returned it was obvious that they had been on a big raid. Four of the braves were dead, draped across their horses. More were wounded. But even while the women of the dead men sent up their wailing and covered their faces with ashes, the rest of the tribe prepared for dancing and celebration.

One of the braves, Francis saw, had a scalp with blond hair. The party must have made a raid against a group of white people, and the only white people in the area were in his wagon train. It sickened him to realize that Braid had probably used *his* rifle to shoot at them.

Braid sought out Francis immediately upon the return of the raiding party.

"They will not be coming for you," the wiry Indian said smirking. "Not now, not ever. I have given them reason to fear the Pawnees. They will not risk fighting us for one stupid little white-eyes."

Francis knew he was telling the truth. They would not be coming for him. Not because they feared these Indians, but because they would think he was dead. The train would lick its wounds and head on for Oregon without him. He would have to find a way to escape on his own.

But Braid hadn't finished yet. The warrior dug into his buckskins, pulled out something, and threw it down in front of Francis.

"I brought this for a girl child," he said. "But perhaps you would enjoy playing with it more."

Francis stared at the object in the dirt. Only one thing kept him from screaming and attacking Braid —and that was the knowledge that it would do no good.

What Braid had thrown down was a small china doll. It was a pretty doll, fashioned after a woman going to a ball.

There was only one thing wrong with the doll— its nose had been broken off. Francis remembered exactly how that had happened. He had been teasing Rebecca, as he did sometimes, and in a fit of anger she had thrown the doll at him. She had missed him, and the doll had hit the corner of the stove and the nose had broken off. It was his sister's doll—Rebecca's doll.

That night, during the dancing and celebration, Francis tried to escape. They caught him not ten feet from the lodge and tied him up.

The next morning they let him loose, and that evening he tried to get away again. This time his "mother" beat him across the backs of his legs with a dried willow cane.

So Francis gave up the idea of escaping for a while. They were watching him too closely.

After his third week there, a large council meeting was held and the tribe decided to move the village. Francis had to help dismantle the lodge and load it on the travois in back of the horses—normally considered woman work, as was gathering wood—but he didn't mind because the work took his mind off the terrible situation he was in.

He did mind the direction the band took when they had finished packing, however. Strung in a long line, with much barking of camp dogs, the file headed due northeast—away from the direction of the wagon train.

I'll have to get all the way to Oregon, Francis thought glumly as he trudged along beside the travois, before I'll find out about Rebecca. That is, if I find a way to escape.

It didn't cheer him either to find that the movement of the tribe—almost twenty miles a day—almost doubled the speed that the wagon train made.

They traveled for ten days, and then put up a new camp on the southern edge of the Black Hills, the village winter ground—the place of sweet water and good hunting.

Strangely, Francis liked the Black Hills even more than he had liked the Rockies. The Black Hills were not only fine to look at—with their dark ridges and green meadows—but good to live with as well.

And it was here that Francis met Mr. Grimes.

It happened early one morning. Francis had just finished fetching wood and was bending down over the fire, built outside the lodge because the days were still quite warm, when it seemed every dog in camp started barking at once. Francis turned to see what all the noise was about, and there, riding into the middle of the Pawnee camp as though it were the main street of St. Louis, was a white man with only one arm.

It was, Francis learned from one of the Indian boys, Mr. Jason Grimes.

Chapter Four

THERE ARE CERTAIN THINGS that are always easy to remember because of the way they happen. Francis's first sight of Mr. Jason Grimes was like that. He would remember it always because of the way Mr. Grimes ignored the Pawnees. It was not an easy thing to do. The Indian dogs were snapping at the hooves of his horses and pack mules, and the squaws and children were so thick all around him that he only showed from the waist up. Yet he ignored them, threading his horse carefully, gracefully around the noisy women and children, looking off in space as though they didn't exist. He made quite a figure as he rode, straight backed, moving easily with the horse's roll. Francis got more of an impression of a piece of timber bolted to a saddle than a man—until he looked at Mr. Grimes's face. It was a thin face, and almost as dark as an Indian's, except that it bore a bushy beard and mustache. He had thin lips and washed-out blue eyes, and on top of his head he wore a dashing but dusty derby, set slightly back, with one long feather sticking straight up from the band. He had on fringed but otherwise not very fancy buckskins, plain moccasins, and no belt.

The last thing Francis noted was that Mr. Grimes's left arm was gone. He carried his rifle, wrapped in a buckskin case, with the same hand that loosely held his horse's reins, and the fact that he had no left arm didn't seem to bother him at all. It seemed almost natural, as though he would have looked odd *with* a left arm.

Francis realized suddenly that he was staring with his mouth open. He shut it. He moved forward through the crowd around the mountain man.

"Hey," he called. "Hey, over here. I'm a *captive*!" The word sounded funny when he said it, but he saw that the mountain man had heard, for he looked down from his horse quickly, then back up.

Francis wasn't sure, but he thought the derby-topped head had shaken left to right just once—as though telling him to be quiet.

Then he couldn't see anything more because his "mother" found him and dropped a noose over his head. She dragged him back, cackling happily, and led him into a corner of the lodge.

With his hands tied in back of him and his ankles lashed firmly together, Francis had plenty of time to think. Most of his thoughts were about the mountain man. How could he come into the Pawnee camp and not be harmed? And *why* had he come? Was he a friend of the Indians?

There were no answers in that dark corner of the lodge, but one thing was plain. The Pawnee weren't going to kill the mountain man. Just the opposite—his arrival was to be the reason for a full day of celebrating. Francis heard all the preparations, and with this knowledge, his heart sank. Any man that friendly with the Pawnees wouldn't be likely to offer him help in escaping.

All that day he lay in the lodge, wondering. He got no food and no water. By nine that night, when the dancing had reached its full frenzy, he at last fell asleep.

Francis wasn't sure of the time when he opened his eyes, but it was either very late that same night or very early the following morning. He did know why he had awakened. There was a calloused hand clamped over his mouth, and in the darkness of the lodge, he could make out the shape of a derby.

It was the mountain man.

Francis felt the bushy beard against his ear, and heard a whisper.

"Don't move. No sound. Just blink your eyes if you hear me and are wide awake."

Francis blinked, and the hand was taken off his mouth.

"Can you ride?" the mountain man asked, still whispering hoarsely.

Francis nodded.

"Good. In back of the lodge you'll find a little black mare I swiped from the Pawnee herd. Walk her out of camp with your hand over her muzzle. When you're safely out of camp, get on her and ride as hard as you can with the North Star on your right shoulder—" He stopped suddenly as Francis's "mother," across the lodge, turned in her sleep. In a second he continued, "If you ride hard enough, and don't hit a hole somewhere, dawn will catch you at a small creek. Take the mare right into the middle of the creek and head upstream. Keep going in the water until you think you're going to drop, then go another ten miles. If you stop, they'll get you. Now, did you understand all that?"

Francis nodded again, "Where will you be?" he asked, rubbing his wrists, which the mountain man had cut loose while he was talking.

"Why, I'll be sitting right here in camp," the mountain man answered, chuckling softly, "eating a good breakfast, wondering whether or not they've caught you. If they don't, I'll see you in a couple of days. Now, are you going to sit and jaw all night or get riding?"

Francis took it for the command it was. Thirty seconds later he was leading the little mare quietly out of the village hoping with all his heart that he smelled enough like an Indian not to upset the dogs.

A minute after that he was on her back, wishing he'd never told a lie in his life. The only time he'd ever been on a horse was when he'd ridden a work-horse while his father plowed. That had only been at a walk, and with a lot of harness straps to hang on to.

The little black mare didn't even have a blanket on her back and she only had two speeds—dead stop and full run.

Chapter Five

FRANCIS GOT HIS FIRST MOUTHFUL of dirt not a hundred paces from where he got on the little black mare. Luckily, he had figured on falling off, and had taken the precaution of wrapping her jaw rope tightly around his hand. When he hit the ground, she dragged him only a couple of yards. He didn't have time to moan about his scraped elbows and knees. He didn't have time for anything but to get on again.

The second time he made nearly three hundred shattering yards before sliding off her side and bouncing on the rocks of a dry streambed. The trouble was that the mare was so fat—it was like trying to ride a nail keg.

He didn't discover the secret until he had fallen off three more times, removing more and more skin from his elbows and knees each time. Then he remembered how the mountain man had ridden—stiff backed, but loose, almost relaxed, where he joined the horse. Francis still bounced around a lot, but all his bouncing was straight up and down—not off to the side. And once he'd learned to relax, Francis found riding the black mare exciting.

Never had he been so purely thrilled. Her dainty head came down, her ears folded back along her flattened neck, and she really flew. Francis didn't try to turn her, as long as she kept in the right general direction—due west—and he forgot everything in the roar of wind and drumming thunder of her hoofs.

Just at false dawn, when the first grayness made faint shadows under trees, the mare streaked out onto a large meadow. It was entirely flat, and she picked up speed when she hit its edge. Francis, content in the knowledge that she wouldn't have to dodge around rocks and trees for a while, relaxed even more and loosened his hold on her mane.

When she hit the water, he went off over her

head, and when he got up, found he was neck deep in muck. The creek ran straight down the middle of the meadow. When he finally managed to scrape the mud from his eyes, the mare was nowhere to be seen. He had dropped the jaw rope, and she had gone on. He couldn't even hear her hooves. He wanted to look for her, then realized he hadn't time for that. This was the stream the mountain man had been talking about. Horse or not, his orders had been definite—head up the middle of the stream, and don't stop.

He stepped deeper into the water, but didn't start upstream immediately. He felt sad that the mare was gone. He would have liked to keep her awhile, and though he didn't think much of the Pawnees he admired their horses.

"Thank you," he said quietly, looking off into the darkness. "Thank you, little mare. It was a good ride."

And he started walking in the water, only vaguely aware of the chill.

Real dawn caught him nearly four miles up the stream. He had long since left the meadow behind, and the stream was now bordered by thick scrub pine trees. He was very tired, and ached all over from his many falls from the mare. But he knew that if he stopped before getting far enough upstream, he might not meet the mountain man again.

So he kept walking; not in miles, or even yards, but in steps. All day long he did that. He quit thinking of food early in the morning; it did nothing but make him hungry. And somehow, without his having been aware of the passing of a day, evening found him still trudging, still moving. He didn't know how far he'd come, only hoped it was far enough.

Just as the first night birds began dipping and wheeling over the stream for insects, Francis Alphonse Tucket pulled himself onto the bank beneath a clump of overhanging willows and dropped like a bag of sand.

In five seconds, wet clothes and all, he wouldn't have heard the Indians even if they beat their drums right next to his head.

Chapter Six

FRANCIS AWAKENED to a heavenly smell—the aroma of boiling coffee. He was afraid that if he opened his eyes, the smell of coffee would vanish. But when a full ten seconds had passed, and the smell was still there, he knew he hadn't been dreaming.

He sat up and saw the mountain man sitting over a small fire about ten feet away. His back was to Francis, but he spoke at once without turning around.

" 'Bout time you opened up a mite—day's half gone already. You sleep like a fancy city man."

Francis stretched, wincing at the pain in his legs. That would be from the little mare, and the pain in his arms would be from falling on them, and the pain in his knees from the rocks he had landed on, but the pain in his stomach was from hunger. "How did you know I was awake?" he asked after a moment.

"Your breathing changed. When you quit sucking wind like an old buffalo, I figured you were coming around."

"You've sure got good ears."

"I'm alive. You don't stay that way long out here unless you can hear a little."

Francis filed away that advice, and got up. Everything in him hurt with the movement. He didn't believe anything could be that stiff and still be alive.

"I thought you said you could ride." The mountain man chuckled.

"I did all right," Francis answered defensively.

"If you mean you made it alive, I guess you did at that. But I wouldn't call what happened to your hands and knees all right. Seems to me you lost a little hide. Still, you pulled a good trick with that mare—sending her off ahead while you came upstream." His chuckle turned to an outright laugh. "I followed Braid and five or six others for a while when they came after you. Unless I miss my guess, they're down on the Powder River somewhere, *still* after that mare."

"I didn't plan it," Francis cut in. "I fell off."

"Eh?"

"I said I fell off her when she hit the stream. I fell off and she kept right on going without me."

"That's sort of what I figured, but I thought it would be better if you said it. Kinda keep the air clean around here, if we talk straight." He turned and faced Francis for the first time. "You know, that lie about knowing how to ride could have got us both killed last night, don't you? They could have caught you, and worked you over a bit, and the first thing you know you would have been telling them all about my getting a horse for you. Don't go shaking your head. I know you wouldn't want to talk. But I've seen the Pawnees make a man tell stories he didn't even *know*. So from now on you just tell me what you know is straight, and that'll keep us *both* out of trouble. What's your name?"

"Francis Alphonse Tucket."

"I said it would be better if we kept everything *straight*, boy. Now what's your handle?"

"I wasn't lying. My name really *is* Francis Alphonse Tucket. Honest."

"Let me put it another way. What do you go by? I mean, haven't you got a sort of short name they call you?"

Francis thought a minute, then shook his head. "My mother always called me Alphonse, and my father called me Francis. I guess you can take your pick."

The trapper shook his head. "I'm sorry, and nothing against your folks, understand, but I don't like either of them. They don't hit my tongue right. Tell you what. My name is Jason Grimes. You call me Mr. Grimes, and I'll call you Mr. Tucket—that should keep us both happy. Is that all right with you?"

Francis shrugged. "Suits me fine, Mr. Grimes."

"Good. Now then, Mr. Tucket, why don't you hobble your crippled body over here and have a sip of coffee? There's nothing like a touch of coffee to take the sharp edge off an empty belly. After that I'll give you a little venison jerky, and while you're chewing that you can tell me how you came to be the son of that old Pawnee lady."

Francis had tried coffee before, stolen from his mother's stove with sugar in it and he took some in a gulp. It was bitter and he nearly spit it out. But the heat of it felt good and seemed to take away some of the ache in his stomach.

The jerky was as tough as an old boot. While he chewed it—and it took *some* chewing—he told Mr. Grimes about the adventure, starting with the wagon train and the rifle.

He finished his tale by telling how Braid had thrown the doll down in front of him.

Mr. Grimes nodded when Francis finished. "That Braid is a mean one. Back before I made friends with the Pawnees by bringing them powder and lead every time I came through, Braid and I had one bush-ripper of a fight. Knives, hatchets—the whole works. I guess it lasted over an hour, and when it was done, he had one scar down his back and I had lost an arm."

"You mean Braid took your arm off?" Francis asked.

"No, he just cut it good. But it got infected later and I had a doctor in St. Louis whack it off before it poisoned my whole body. It makes for some pretty tight talking whenever I come into his village. Braid hasn't forgotten his scar a bit, and every time I come in he asks me to wrestle. Oh, and speaking of wrestling, I've got something for you. Won it from Braid yesterday wrestling—he made the mistake of tying one arm behind his back to make the fight more fair. He was too stupid to realize that I get a lot of all kinds of practice with only one arm, so I whipped him pretty easy."

As he talked, Mr. Grimes went to his saddle and pulled out a blanket wrapped around something. He carefully unrolled the blanket and handed Francis his rifle, mold, powder, and caps.

"My rifle!"

"Yup, and a sweet little shooter she is, too. I knew it was yours when you started telling me about getting it for your birthday. Seeing as how it looks like we'll be riding together for a while—at least until I teach you enough so's you can make Oregon on your own—we'll take a couple of days off and I'll teach you to shoot it."

"I can shoot," Francis said.

"Well, maybe you can, and maybe you can't. But just reading signs makes your story look thin."

"What do you mean?" Francis asked.

"I mean if you *really* knew how to shoot that rifle, it wouldn't have been seven Pawnees jumping you that day by the wagon train. It would only have been five, and maybe just four—and those four would have been thinking seriously about going home without you. *That's* what I mean."

Chapter Seven

"NO-AH, MR. TUCKET, that isn't quite the way it's done."

It was the first time Mr. Grimes used the long, drawn-out negative answer to something Francis had messed up. But it wasn't to be the last. In fact, he would use that long no, as Francis thought of it, about ten times to every short nod, which was the way the mountain man approved of anything.

It was the afternoon of the day Francis and Mr. Grimes had met at the stream. Francis had just loaded and fired his gun as instructed by Mr.

Grimes. He felt that he'd done all right. A piece of wood more than thirty yards distant had turned to splinters with his shot. And it *had* been the piece of wood he was shooting at.

"What did I do wrong?" he asked. "I hit the piece of wood, didn't I?" There was just a thin bit of annoyance in his voice.

Mr. Grimes smiled and hooked his right hand in back of his neck, stretching. "Well, now, that's just about what *everybody* says—when they don't know about rifles." He mimicked Francis, " 'I hit the piece of wood, didn't I?' And yes, you did, Mr. Tucket. You hit the piece of wood. But how many times more can you hit it? Go ahead, load up and have at it. Pick another piece of wood out there and hit it for me, will you?"

Francis loaded, aimed, and fired at a buffalo chip about forty yards away. He missed. He tried twice more and missed both times.

Mr. Grimes nodded. "It's this way. You're holding that thing like it was an old rag. Your arms are loose, you're slopping your cheek against the stock, you're grabbing with your hands—and that's all wrong. You'll hit once or twice that way, if you're lucky. But the real trick of shooting a decent gun is to be able to put about four out of five balls in the same place, or nearly so. Now, Mr. Tucket, we'll see if we can't do a little reshaping of that crippled body of yours . . ."

He wasn't fooling. In the next five minutes Francis felt as though both his arms had been broken. Mr. Grimes pulled Francis's right elbow up so high the shoulder popped, and he jerked the left elbow down, directly beneath the barrel of the rifle.

"And don't grab with that left hand on the stock. Just make a baby cradle with your fingers and let the rifle sleep in it."

Francis nodded. It hurt, standing that way, but he could see how it made for more consistent shooting.

"All right, Mr. Tucket, load up and fire again."

Francis didn't start hitting right away, but at least his shots were falling in the same general area. He turned after four shots. "How's that?"

Mr. Grimes nodded. "All right, but you're taking too long to reload."

"What do you mean, too long? It was just a couple of seconds between shots." Actually it was more like a minute. But that wasn't what Mr. Grimes meant.

"It's this way, Mr. Tucket. What would you do if Braid came riding up the creek right now?"

"Why, I'd . . ." Francis blushed. He was standing with an empty rifle. If Braid, or any other threat, for that matter, came riding up the creek, Francis knew it would take him at least thirty seconds to load.

"That's right, Mr. Tucket. You'd be tied like a cow before you got powder down the bore. Every time you shoot, no matter whether you're shooting at buffalo chips or buffalo, you load as soon as the ball leaves the barrel. Carrying an empty rifle is about like carrying an empty water skin. When you get really thirsty, Mr. Tucket, you can't drink air."

Francis smiled sheepishly. "I guess I've got a lot to learn, haven't I?"

"Ayup, Mr. Tucket, you have a lot to learn, but you're coming along. Now let's clean that little shooter of yours and try some rapid firing. That's what really separates the men, or boys, for that matter, from their scalps in this country—not being able to shoot *fast.*"

Cleaning the rifle was easy. Francis just cupped creek water in his hand and poured it down the barrel, swabbed it with a piece of patch on the end of his ramrod, then greased the bore.

"Now this is how we'll do it," Mr. Grimes told him, fetching his own rifle from his saddle. "We'll have a sort of contest. We'll start at the same time, and the one who gets the most shots off while I count to ten will get out of working tonight—getting wood and cooking some of the jerky. Does that suit you, Mr. Tucket?"

Francis nodded. He didn't see how he could lose, shooting against a one-armed man.

"All right, Mr. Tucket. Go!"

"But you don't even have your rifle out of its case, Mr. Grimes," Francis said. "You aren't even ready."

"Just giving you the benefit of a little head start, Mr. Tucket. Ready? Go!"

They both fired at the same instant. Mr. Grimes had just flipped his rifle and fired, one-armed, before its buckskin case hit the ground.

"One," he said, starting the count.

Francis worked frantically. From his flask he poured powder into his cupped palm, then he emptied the roughly measured powder down the bore.

"Two."

As Francis was placing the patch across the mouth of the bore, he heard the roar of Mr. Grimes's Hawkens. He couldn't believe it. He put the ball on the patch, and drew the ramrod from its cradle beneath the barrel. He started the ball down with his thumb . . .

"Three."

. . . and put the ramrod on top of it. As he slammed the ball home he heard the mighty

Hawkens roar again. Mr. Grimes had fired three to his one. Francis capped the nipple, raised the rifle . . .

"Four."

. . . and fired. As his second shot tore a buffalo chip to pieces, the Hawkens belched fire a fourth time. It was too much for Francis. He lowered his rifle and watched Mr. Grimes.

"Five."

Mr. Grimes raised his Hawkens and fired. Number five. Five shots in the time it had taken Francis to make two. Clearly, Francis had missed something.

"Six."

Mr. Grimes lowered the Hawkens and held it between his knees. In one fluid motion he poured powder from the flask at his side down the barrel directly—without measuring—and brought the muzzle of the rifle up to his mouth. From his lips he spit a ball into the muzzle. Without a patch, it slid freely down, needing no ramrod. He slammed the butt of the rifle on the ground, to seat the ball, and from the space between his fingers pulled a percussion cap. It fitted quickly on the nipple, the Hawkens came up, and . . .

"Seven."

. . . smoke again poured out over the grass.

Mr. Grimes lowered his rifle and grinned. "I don't guess I have to go all the way to ten after all."

"But that wasn't fair," Francis said. "You didn't patch your balls, or measure your powder—"

"Now, now, Mr. Tucket. The word 'fair' is pretty loose. What's not fair in St. Louis at a turkey shoot might *be* fair when you're up against five or six Comanch." He cut the word "Comanche" off. "Out here people sort of think of 'fair' meaning the same as 'alive.' Savvy?"

Francis smiled. "Savvy. 'Fair' means that I'm going to gather wood and cook jerky."

"You *are* coming along, Mr. Tucket," the mountain man said, grinning again. "Ten, fifteen years, if you're still alive, you'll be the best wood gatherer in the Black Hills . . ."

Chapter Eight

THEY LEFT EARLY the next morning. Francis would have liked to stay on for a few more days, but Mr. Grimes saddled his big sorrel gelding just after coffee with the air of a man who has somewhere to go, and Francis, stiff or not, knew better than to make any other suggestions.

"Come on up, Mr. Tucket. Let's see how old Footloose carries double."

As it turned out, old Footloose carried double almost as well as he carried single. Francis was given the job of holding the rope that led back to the pack mules. They followed nicely—showing none of the stubbornness Francis thought mules were supposed to show—and under a lightly clouded sky they made their way at a slow walk toward the southwest.

If Francis had expected a lot of conversation as they rode, he would have been sadly disappointed. Mr. Grimes was of the thinking that when he had something to say, he said it—usually with a bit of pepper thrown in. But when there wasn't anything to talk about, two or three hours might pass without a word coming from his bearded face.

Francis had close to a hundred questions he wanted to ask, but he didn't say anything for nearly two hours. In that time they had passed out of the main part of the pine forests and were winding down a dry-bottom canyon. It was an extremely pleasant place, even without water. Both sides of the canyon were of gray rock, and were high enough to keep the mid-morning sun from reaching Francis's back. Occasionally he could hear magpies chattering, and twice he heard the drumming of grouse, beating their wings on rotten logs. Even the sound of the sorrel's shod hooves, ringing off the rock walls, seemed natural and nice.

There was something bothering Francis, however, that kept him from enjoying these things the way he might have. Part of it was Rebecca—and not knowing about her. But it was Mr. Grimes that upset him more, and finally, as the sorrel brought them out of the canyon and back into the sun, Francis spoke up.

"Mr. Grimes, how is it that you're so friendly with the Pawnees—I mean, with Braid having caused you to lose your arm and all? I would think you'd be downright mad, or at least not friendly enough to bring them powder and lead."

Mr. Grimes snorted, and Francis could see the mountain man's back jerk as he began to laugh. "Honestly, Mr. Tucket, you do ask the mulish questions, don't you? I'll bet you spend the rest of your days looking gift horses in their mouths."

"What do you mean?"

"You want me to answer that? Or would you rather figure it out for yourself?" the mountain man said. "It seems simple to me. If I hadn't been 'friendly with the Pawnees' as you put it, you'd be back there with a rope around your neck, getting whipped."

"I'm sorry," Francis murmured. "It was a dumb thing to ask—"

"But since you asked," Mr. Grimes cut in, "I think maybe I ought to answer it. You think I ought to be mad at Braid on account of my arm. Well, Braid can't help the way he was made, no more than you or me. The Pawnees call themselves 'The People.' They live with the land. If you put it in our talk, that means they live by nature—the same nature that makes a she-bear gut you if you mess with her cubs. Braid costing me my arm is about the same as if a she-bear took it. I couldn't get mad at a bear and I couldn't get mad at Braid, and I couldn't hate the whole Pawnee tribe because of a mistake."

"You call losing an arm a *mistake*?" Francis asked.

"Yes, sir. I should have got Braid before he got my arm—not doing it was a mistake."

"How can you talk about killing Braid when you don't hate him, aren't even mad at him?"

"Now be careful, Mr. Tucket. Asking a question is one thing—even when it's a dumb question. But now you're picking, and picking is what St. Louis city folk do . . ."

"No—I mean it. In the wagon train and at Braid's village, I fought a lot. But I couldn't *really* fight unless I got good and mad. Now you make it all sound so cool and calm—I just don't understand, that's all."

Mr. Grimes laughed. "Let me put it another way. I live by trapping, mostly beaver. Sometimes I trap on Pawnee land, sometimes not. When I *do* trap on Pawnee land, it figures that I'd want to do it without getting my hair lifted, so I bring them something they need—powder and lead—and I don't get mad. I get something—beaver pelts—and the Pawnees get something. We all stay happy. Well, maybe not happy—but alive."

Francis couldn't help himself. "Why do you have to bring them powder and lead? They turn right around and use it on white people—like my folks. That doesn't seem right to me . . ."

Francis felt the trapper stiffen in the saddle. He bit his tongue, and thought that he fully deserved getting knocked on the ground and left for the Indians.

Gradually the stiffness went away. Without turning, and in a dead-even voice, Mr. Grimes said, "I guess we'd better ride quiet for a while."

For nearly an hour there was only the sound of the sorrel's hooves and bird calls and their own breathing. Francis called himself many kinds of a fool in that time.

When the silence was at last broken, it was Mr. Grimes who spoke.

"You've been through a lot in the past month or so, and I guess maybe I ought to take that into consideration a mite—"

"No," Francis interrupted, glad of the chance to

speak. "I was dumb. I'm sorry—I shouldn't have talked that way."

"Well, I'm going to say something to you that I shouldn't have to say. I'm not a war maker. I don't want to kill Pawnees, and I don't want to kill whites. If they want to kill each other, that's something else again. I ride right down the middle. And if my powder and lead is used to kill whites, I'm sorry. But it's not my fault. That same powder and lead would kill a lot of buffalo and antelope—and that's how most of it is used. Some mountain men and traders bring the Indians whiskey—if you want to pick yourself a *real* fight, go after those men."

"But I didn't mean—"

"And don't come clawing at me. I've killed a few Indians in my time, and I'll probably kill a few more. I may even put Braid under, someday, or he may kill me. But you can make money on this: If I *do* kill Braid, it won't be because he has something I want, like land. I'll leave that to the farmers—your people. And that's the last I want to hear about it."

He quit talking as suddenly as he'd begun. Again the silence was thick and painful. There was nothing Francis could say, and he knew it, and the knowledge made him even sadder.

"Mr. Grimes," he asked, "where are we going?"

"You mean today, or next month?"

"Well, today, I guess. I thought if we happened to be going near a settlement of some kind in the next few days, you could drop me off."

The mountain man nodded. "If that's what you want. We'll be getting to a settlement tonight—or at least the only kind of settlement they have out here. You can drop off there if you want to. I think Standing Bear would be right proud to have you stay awhile—"

"Standing Bear?" Francis cut in. "Who's he?"

"He's the head of the settlement. I was thinking earlier of swinging by there and picking up a horse for you. Of course now that you want to stop, we'll just drop in and forget about the horse . . ."

"What kind of a settlement is it?"

"Well, it's not really a settlement. More like what you'd call a camp. Out here we call it something else."

"What do you call it?"

"A village," the mountain man answered, chuckling. "Out here we call it a Sioux village. You sure do pick the funniest places to want to stay, Mr. Tucket."

Chapter Nine

FRANCIS TRIED not to be afraid when the Sioux village came into view. He had seen only one type of Indian so far, the mean type. And he knew that the Pawnee tribe was the not-too-distant cousin of the Sioux. Thoughts of recapture took the place of his faith in Mr. Grimes's judgment, and Francis went cold all over.

"Easy, Mr. Tucket," the mountain man said without turning. "This is like a show. You saw me come into the Pawnee village—we do the same thing here. Act easy."

Francis took his cue from Mr. Grimes. He stiffened his back and tried to remember something not related to where he was now. His mind settled on the birthday cake his mother had made, and looking straight ahead—neither down nor left nor right—he pictured it in exact detail.

The clamor in the village was deafening. Chief Standing Bear's group had an even noisier bunch of dogs than the Pawnees, and the children's howling was earshattering. Francis marveled at the sorrel and the mules. They paid no more attention to the screaming than did their master except that once a mule took aim and nearly drove a dog's head through his rear end with a rear hoof.

Finally, when they had woven their way to about the center of the village, Mr. Grimes pulled lightly on the reins and stopped.

"Standing Bear," the mountain man called.

Francis watched as a small channel opened in the crowd to the right and an Indian, who limped, came through. He was short, bowlegged, and stocky, but he moved with a smoothness that made Francis think immediately of a cat. It must be Standing Bear, Francis thought, and he was not smiling. When he was five feet from the sorrel, his right hand came up slowly, and with as much grace as he used walking.

Mr. Grimes shrugged, said something in Sioux to the chief, received an answer, and laughed.

"I *thought* it was a mite tight," he said to Francis. "Braid sent word ahead and asked Standing Bear to hold you if the Sioux found you. That's interesting since the Pawnee and Sioux are usually enemies—I guess he made a small peace with this village because catching you is so important. It would seem, Mr. Tucket, that you hurt his prestige —the black mare was Braid's personal mount. You sure do things in spades when you get loose, don't you? Taking a war leader's prize horse and all."

"Me?" Francis said. "*I* didn't take—"

"Now, now, Mr. Tucket. Just leave sleeping dogs alone. Old Standing Bear here thinks you must be one go-getter of a young warrior—bucking a big war leader and all. The Sioux think it's the funniest joke they ever heard, so why don't you just play along?"

All the time he had been talking to Francis, Mr. Grimes hadn't stopped looking and smiling at Standing Bear. He said something in Sioux, laughed again when Standing Bear answered, and nodded. "Raise your right hand, Mr. Tucket, the way standing Bear put up his."

Francis complied. "What did you say to him?"

"I told him you were the toughest fighter in the

Black Hills, that you were clever as the fox, that your heart was the heart of a mountain lion."

"You said all that about me?"

"Don't let it go to your head, Mr. Tucket. Indians don't take anybody's word on anything. Standing Bear says that he has a pretty tough boy in *his* village—"

"Oh, no . . ."

"Oh, yes, Mr. Tucket. It seems that your wrestling days aren't over yet." He turned and again said something to Standing Bear in Sioux.

"*Now* what did you tell him?" Francis asked.

"I just said that you weren't afraid of his boy, sort of."

"What do you mean, 'sort of'?"

"I said you were so sure of winning that you'd bet your rifle against a good pony and a set of buckskins."

"You did *what*?"

"Now don't get rattled, Mr. Tucket. Didn't those Pawnee boys teach you *anything* about wrestling?"

Francis's eyes scanned the crowd around them, looking for his possible competitor. "Yes, Mr. Grimes, the Pawnees *did* teach me something about wrestling."

"Well, then . . ."

"They taught me how to lose."

There were certain formalities that had to be observed before the match. Mr. Grimes had also brought the Sioux powder and lead. Francis watched him loosen the pack on one of the mules and remove a small keg. It couldn't have been more than a two-pound keg of powder, but the way the Sioux carried on, it could well have been two hundred pounds of triple-fine.

"They can't make it," Mr. Grimes told Francis. "So the only way they can get powder is to buy it, or get it as a gift, or steal it."

After distributing the powder there was more talk, and *still* more talk with Standing Bear. Francis almost went to sleep on the sorrel just listening to him. By this time all of the women had disappeared, the children had backed out of the circle of men, and Mr. Grimes seemed to be the only one listening to Standing Bear. The sun set while he was talking, the evening chill seeped into Francis's back, fires began to flare up around camp, the smell of buffalo cooking touched his nostrils, and *still* Standing Bear talked on.

Finally the Indian's voice stopped.

Mr. Grimes said something briefly in Sioux. The Indian replied, just as briefly. Mr. Grimes nodded, and turned to Francis. "Better get down and stretch a bit. Footloose is probably tired, too."

Francis slid off to the left and fell flat on his face. Both his legs were asleep.

Mr. Grimes muttered something in Sioux and all the warriors laughed.

"What did you say?" Francis asked.

"I told them you were saving your legs for the match."

"Well, if it hadn't been for old, old chief windbag there, my legs probably wouldn't have fallen asleep," Francis said grumpily, flexing his knees. "What was he talking about, anyway?"

"Well, he said that his lands reach to where it is always cold in the North, to where great waters end the land in the East, as far as all the ducks and geese and small birds fly in the cold of the end of the time of the sun—"

"Couldn't you cut it down a bit?" Francis asked. "I'm hungry."

"He said I could trap beaver on Sioux land. I thanked him. Then he said I was welcome. Then you fell off the horse—"

"All right. I understood that part. Now do I get a chance to eat before I lose my rifle?"

"Sure do, Mr. Tucket, prime buffalo. But I don't know as I like this negative thinking you're doing.

Cheer up a mite. They probably won't have but a midget against you. Why not think instead of owning a pony and some good buckskins?"

"I told you. I'm too good at losing."

Many things were stacked up against Francis's chances of winning the pony and buckskins. First, he was so hungry that when food was finally offered him, in the form of a large slab of hot buffalo meat, he ate until he could barely stand.

Then, too, two days hadn't completely worn out the stiffness in his legs, hips, and arms. And riding all day on the rounded haunch of the sorrel was hardly good training for wrestling. But the main obstacle was the Indian boy Standing Bear had picked to fight him. He was not a midget, he wasn't even small.

Francis stood on one side of a circle of braves. At his side, silent as usual, was Mr. Grimes. Across from him, and just inside the circle, was the Indian boy—a good thirty feet away.

He was about four inches taller than Francis, and he weighed about ten pounds more than Francis's one hundred and thirty-five pounds. And *he* hadn't spent the whole day riding on the sorrel.

"This is going to be murder," Francis whispered to Mr. Grimes. "Pure murder."

"I'm glad to see your confidence returning, Mr.

Tucket. Just a few minutes ago you were ready to give up. Now you're talking about killing him."

"I meant it the other way."

"Oh."

Francis looked across the circle. A large fire had been built to one side, and in the light he could see two men smearing something on the other boy.

"What are they doing to him?" Francis asked.

"Greasing him," Mr. Grimes answered. "And it's about time you took your shirt off."

"You mean I've got to do that?"

"No, you don't, Mr. Tucket. But the grease is going to make it harder to hold him than a wet catfish. It seems sensible to me that you'd sort of feel like doing the same thing."

Francis took off his shirt slowly, and Mr. Grimes covered him from the waist up with cold buffalo grease.

"It stinks," Francis complained.

"Don't say that too loud." Mr. Grimes chuckled. "They think it smells nice—like perfume."

More wood was thrown on the fire. Into the center of the circle stepped Standing Bear. He looked first at the Indian boy and seemed to snort something in Sioux. The Indian boy smiled and nodded. Standing Bear turned to Francis and snorted the same thing.

"Nod and grin," Mr. Grimes told him. "He's asking if you're ready."

Francis nodded and smiled, at least halfheartedly. He didn't really feel ready.

Standing Bear snorted some more, then spoke for a full five minutes.

"He's spouting the rules," Mr. Grimes said. "No biting, no hitting with the closed hand, no hitting with elbows or knees, humph, I didn't know that."

"Know what?"

"They allow kicking, but not with the toes. You have to curve your toes under and kick with the top of your foot. I guess you'd better take your boots off, Mr. Tucket. It wouldn't be fair to kick him with boots on."

Francis sighed resignedly and stooped to remove his boots. You might know they'd allow kicking, he thought. In truth, his boots were in tatters, but he felt odd barefoot.

"The rest of the rules are simple. You fight in the circle and stay out of the fire. If one of you falls or is thrown out of the circle, he gets thrown right back in and the fight goes on. The match ends when one of you says uncle—go." Mr. Grimes pushed Francis into the ring. The other boy had already entered from the other side.

Francis had wrestled a lot with the Pawnee boys, but he was hardly ready for this Sioux terror. With a loud scream the Indian boy, grinning widely, bounced across the clearing, spun lightly on his left leg, and placed the instep of his right foot dead in the center of Francis's still-undigested buffalo, hard.

It was a kick solid enough to drop an ox. Francis went down with his hands doubled over his stomach and a look of complete surprise on his face.

The Sioux boy landed on him like a cougar—a smiling cougar—and Francis's arm was twisted up his back and his face was mashed in the dirt.

A loud collective grunt issued from around the circle. It was going to be a quick fight, and the Sioux boy would have a fine new rifle. This white boy must have been terribly lucky in his dealings with the warrior Braid.

But Francis wasn't quitting, in spite of being out of breath, and having a mouth full of dirt. The arm lock looked wicked but it didn't hurt much. The Indian had failed to twist the arm enough to make it painful, and his mistake gave Francis much needed time to catch his breath. Then he used a trick he'd learned fighting with Max. He totally and completely relaxed, even the arm the Indian boy was holding. It worked. The Sioux wrestler felt the relaxing, and took the opportunity to change his hold.

It was what Francis had hoped for. With a mighty heave, he arched his back upward and threw the Sioux boy. Then he scrambled and landed, as hard as he could, on top of the boy, grabbed him around the neck and leg, and arched his back.

Another grunt came from the crowd. Maybe the fight would go on for a while yet. Francis heard Mr. Grimes on the side: "Well done, Mr. Tucket."

In almost any other match it would have been the end, for the Indian was all but paralyzed. Francis was on the boy's back, pulling him up at both ends, and he couldn't move.

But because of the grease, Francis couldn't maintain his hold. His hand slipped from the boy's neck, the Indian rolled over, and before Francis really knew what had happened, *he* was in the dirt.

This time Francis saw something new in the Indian's eyes. It was respect. Whereas he had jumped in screaming the first time, he now circled warily as the two regained their feet.

This was Francis's kind of fighting. The circling, looking for a weakness, was how he had learned to wrestle with white boys, and he noticed now a weakness in the Indian. He favored his right leg, the one Francis had twisted.

It was simple, then. All Francis had to do was feint to the left, then come in hard on the right.

The Indian boy would be slow that way, and Francis could get a neck hold, usually a match-stopper.

He feinted, and came in on the right, and the Indian boy was waiting for him. The weak leg had been only a bait, and Francis ran straight into a backhanded slap across his windpipe. It stopped his breathing again, and in the brief second that he hesitated, the Indian tripped him and used Francis's own hold—the reverse back arch. But there was a new twist. Instead of grabbing Francis around the neck, the Indian boy wrapped his fingers in Francis's hair, where there was no grease.

Still another grunt came from the crowd. Surely this would be the end of the match. The white boy couldn't move, and he couldn't get away. Some of the men even turned to go back to their lodges.

Francis *couldn't* move. He tried relaxing again, but the trick didn't work a second time. The Indian boy had him. It wasn't over, though, after all. Mr. Grimes leaned over from the edge of the circle and whispered: "Mr. Tucket, there's been talk of keeping you for Braid if you don't put up a better fight."

Francis didn't really believe him. It was the sort of thing Mr. Grimes would say just to get him riled. But he wasn't quite sure. The Indians did some funny things, and the thought of being sent back to Braid's camp was a terrible thought.

The Indian boy did something completely natural. He spat to get the dust out of his mouth. He didn't spit at or on Francis. But the spit landed about four inches in front of his eyes.

Francis saw pink, then red, and finally just fire. "Now you didn't have to go and do *that*," he yelled in English.

Later not even Mr. Grimes could tell how Francis got out of the hold. But get out of the hold he did, and within thirty seconds it was pretty clear to the crowd that one angry white boy was going to be a pony and a set of buckskins richer. His twist to get out of the hold knocked the Indian boy on his back in the dirt, and Francis, acting more from instinct than logic, made what Mr. Grimes later called a "goat leap." He jumped high in the air and, in an almost perfect swan dive, landed headfirst in the center of the Indian's stomach. Before the boy could regain his breath, Francis had flopped down and wrapped a scissors hold around his chest. Five seconds passed, then ten, and on the fifteenth second—Mr. Grimes had been counting—the Indian boy gasped his defeat. "That's enough, Mr. Tucket," Mr. Grimes called.

Francis released the boy immediately, no longer angry. He stood, and was surprised to see the Indian boy smiling up at him. On the spur of the moment, he leaned down and helped the still-gasping boy to get up. Around the circle there were many grunts of approval.

The Indian, as soon as his breathing settled down, began jabbering and laughing right away. Francis turned to Mr. Grimes.

"What's he saying?"

"He's saying it was well worth a pony to learn that new trick—he means that business of butting."

"Well, I'm glad he's happy," Francis said, laughing also. "And you can tell him that I learned something myself." He rubbed his back. "I may have won a pony, but I don't think I'll be riding it right away . . ."

—— Chapter Ten ——

FRANCIS COULDN'T FIGURE OUT what to do. First he decided he wanted to stay on at Standing Bear's village, but then he found that he wanted to go on with Mr. Grimes. He had announced that he wouldn't be able to ride the pony for a while, but even so Mr. Grimes shook him awake at dawn the next morning.

"Come on, Mr. Tucket. There's a horse to be picked out, and we have to be on our way today. I swear, you sleep like a bear in winter."

Actually, there wasn't "a horse to be picked

out." Standing Bear had already done the picking—and true to Indian form, he had chosen the best pony in the corral.

She was a mare, and except for a white splotch of hair across her rump in the shape of a bird's wing, she was as black as the night. Standing Bear pointed to her with pride, smiled, and talked in Sioux to Mr. Grimes, who reported to Francis:

"He says he picked the pony for two reasons. One, she is good. Two, he hears you have a special liking for black mares. That's a joke and you should laugh."

Francis laughed.

Standing Bear talked some more.

"He says that she's been trained to hunt buffalo, and you should steer her with you knees. Nod and smile."

Francis nodded and smiled at the chief. It wasn't what he'd normally call a smiling morning. The sun wasn't warm yet, he hadn't gone to sleep until well past midnight, and he wouldn't have made it from his borrowed buffalo-robe bed to the corral if Mr. Grimes hadn't half dragged him. It seemed like all he had done since getting lost from the wagon train was get stiffer and stiffer.

Standing Bear acknowledged Francis's smile. He said something in Sioux.

"The pony is now yours," Mr. Grimes translated. "You can take her to your lodge—I guess he means where you slept last night, up by old Footloose."

The mare had a rope halter. Francis opened the corral gate and tried to grab the halter. She backed away, mixing in with some other ponies. He looked questioningly at Mr. Grimes. "How do I catch her?"

"You could run her down," the mountain man answered.

Francis gave him a nasty look. He could barely walk. At that moment, Mr. Grimes stepped into the corral with a horsehide rope. He flipped it out once, twice, and on the third try the noose fell over the mare's head. She stopped then at the feel of the rope on her neck and Francis hobbled up to her.

"Come on, Mr. Tucket," said the mountain man. "Climb on. Let's see how she takes to your weight."

"But, Mr. Grimes . . ." Francis complained. "I'm like a board. Give me a day or two to loosen up—"

"The best way to loosen up is to move a bit. Now climb on, before Standing Bear gets the thought you don't *like* his pony."

All the time he had been talking, Mr. Grimes

was fashioning from a second piece of rope a war bridle—a slipknot—around the mare's lower jaw.

In two tries, Francis managed to get his stomach over the back of the mare. He swiveled slowly until his legs hung down either side, then sat up, straight and stiff.

"Please, little pony," he said quietly, "remember my condition."

The strange part was that the pony *did* seem to understand. She didn't move quickly, or buck, or even tremble. And when Mr. Grimes handed him the end of the war-bridle rope, she walked toward the gate as meekly as a kitten.

It was Standing Bear who caused the trouble. Just as Francis and the pony came through the gate, the Sioux chief picked up a switch, moved behind the mare, and brought the switch down across the white splotch on her rump.

"Eeeeyah!" he yelled.

Actually, as Mr. Grimes pointed out later, Francis should have thanked the old chief, because what happened next loosened Francis in a hurry. But when that switch landed, he was too surprised to do anything but grab the mane of the black mare and close his eyes.

The mare became a dark comet, flashing through the middle of the awakening Sioux village like a fast wind. She knocked dogs out of the way and cleared cooking fires—jumping completely over one old woman kneeling over a pot of food. Through all this, Francis managed somehow to stay on her back.

When the mare reached the edge of the village, she stopped. Francis naturally kept on going, and finally *he* stopped with his face buried in a pile of still raw buffalo hides, but his troubles weren't over yet.

Coming hot on the heels of the little mare was the old woman, throwing rocks as fast as she could. Francis might be a good wrestler, and very smart to outwit Braid—but *nobody* jumped a horse over the old woman and her cook fire and got away with it.

Francis was quick to recognize disaster. Forgetting the mare, he made a dash back toward the safety of Mr. Grimes.

Mr. Grimes wasn't offering much safety. In fact, he wasn't offering anything. He and Standing Bear were wrapped over the top of the pole of the corral, laughing till tears ran down their cheeks.

"Keep it up, Mr. Tucket," the trapper said, as Francis ran by. "She's gaining on you."

Within a hundred yards Francis outran the old woman *and* her deadly rocks, and had also managed to kick away about ten of the camp dogs that had been snapping at his heels.

"Jokers," he mumbled, returning to the corral. The mare had walked back, looking as meek as she had before the wild ride. "Real jokers. I bet you get a lot of laughs out of throwing people off cliffs."

"Now, Mr. Tucket. Old Standing Bear just wanted you to know you were getting a pony that knew how to *run*." The mountain man was barely holding back laughter. "Besides, look how loose you are. You might as well be an old washrag . . ."

Francis nodded, looking down at himself. "And I look like one, too." But his anger weakened fast, and he smiled. The truth was he *had* loosened up.

"We'll stop early today," Mr. Grimes said. "I feel like some fresh antelope. And you can just carry your buckskins until then, so you can take a bath and start all new."

"I guess I will go with you," Francis said.

"Oh. Well, that depends, Mr. Tucket."

"On what?"

"On whether or not you can spend half a day riding downwind of me. You smell positively ripe from those hides."

── Chapter Eleven ──

NOON FOUND THE TWO RIDERS almost ten miles from the Sioux village. They were on the edge of a small stream, and Francis was only too glad when Mr. Grimes called a halt at a clearing.

"While you're stripping and taking a bath," the mountain man said, "I'll scout up ahead for some meat. There's a mesa about two miles on down where there's usually an antelope or two."

Francis nodded. They picketed the mules, and Mr. Grimes rode off.

Warm, with little or no breeze dancing through

the cottonwoods along the stream, it was truly a day made for swimming. Francis hit the water before the mountain man was out of sight. It was cold—spring fed in the hills somewhere—but the cold only made it all the more refreshing. He played around for a while, diving and splashing in a deep pool, and then scrubbed himself, using his shirt for a washcloth.

He climbed out of the stream and let the sun dry him as he lay on his back. He'd come a long way, he thought. Not in miles—he doubted that he was much closer to Oregon than when the Pawnees had captured him. But in time and knowledge, he'd come what seemed like a thousand years. He'd seen and done more than most people did all their lives, and he was only fourteen.

Presently he was dry, so he unwrapped the buckskins from one of the mule packs on the ground. They were plain, like Mr. Grimes's, and for the same reason. You could hide easier without a lot of colored beads to give you away. Actually, the buckskins had been made as a hunting suit for the boy he had wrestled. But they were new and hadn't been used yet and they fit Francis. The pants stopped at his ankles and fitted tightly to his hips and legs—following the principle of most Indian dress that a belt was good for nothing but cutting into your stomach when you bent over. The buckskin shirt had one set of fringes across the chest, was open at the throat, and its bottom fell almost a foot below his waist.

Mr. Grimes had thought ahead. There were no pockets in the buckskins, so he had procured for Francis a "possibles" sack to hold his flask and shooting equipment. This hung from a strap over his shoulder. Mr. Grimes had also picked up a pair of plain, ankle-high moccasins for him.

When Francis finished dressing, he looked nothing like the boy who had left St. Louis with the wagon train. The buckskins, even new, gave him the appearance of belonging more to the plains than to a settlement. His face was weathered and tan, and his hair—usually kept short by his mother—fell well below his ears.

He smiled, thinking of how he must look. It's too bad I don't have a mirror, he told himself. I probably look like a young Mr. Grimes. The idea strangely pleased him, and his smile widened as he carried his old clothes across the stream and buried them beneath a rotten log. He felt as though he was burying his past life.

He came back across the stream just as Mr. Grimes returned. He stopped the sorrel but did not dismount.

"Well, well, Mr. Tucket. I near mistook you for Jim Bridger. Probably would have if you didn't have brown hair. Jim is turning gray at the temples."

Francis felt a blush sweep over his face.

Mr. Grimes didn't miss it. "I was going to ask you to shoot an antelope for me—but now I don't know. A red face stands out just a mite, and you might scare them away. Howsomever, if you can pull yourself up on the mare one more time, maybe I can offer you a little sport."

Francis wheeled away, glad for the chance to do something. Mr. Grimes had the darndest way of *noticing* everything. Francis untied the mare, slipped her war bridle up tight, and with his rifle in one hand, jumped on her back. He took the reins in his other hand.

Mr. Grimes loped out of camp and Francis jabbed his heels into the mare's ribs to catch up. They rode side by side for twenty minutes, and then pulled up sharply on the edge of what Francis first took to be a cliff. Below them lay an immense level plain, as green as a hay field and twice as flat. Far out on the opposite side of the mesa Francis could see fifteen or twenty brown specks.

"Antelope, Mr. Tucket—or dinner, depending on how you look at it. I'd like you to shoot me a nice young buck—"

"From *here*?" Francis interrupted. "Why, they're at least two miles away."

"No-ah, Mr. Tucket. Not from here. You leave your mare up here with me and you climb down there. Then you hide and"—he dug in his saddle-bags and produced a piece of white cloth—"and wave this around for a while. It's an old Indian trick. They get curious about what you're wiggling and come to see what it is. *Then* you shoot one—and make sure he's a young buck. The old ones get old by running a lot—and that makes them tough."

Francis took the rag, slid off his horse, and looked down the cliff. Actually it was a steep slide, and could be descended fairly easily.

"Why are you sending me down?" he asked. "I've never shot an antelope . . ."

"That's just why, Mr. Tucket. That's just why. Now you'd better get going—we've only got about seven hours of daylight left." His voice was sarcastic.

Francis looked across the mesa at the antelope and shrugged. He was sure asked to do a lot of funny things. He started down the slide.

Going down was easy, and it wasn't as far as it looked. In fifteen minutes he was at the bottom, in back of a small rise, and lying on his stomach waving the rag in the air.

Francis couldn't see the antelope, and as the seconds turned into minutes, he wasn't completely sure that the antelope could see his waving rag. He raised carefully up on his elbows in the grass, but could see nothing. Turning, he looked up at the slide—hoping to see Mr. Grimes calling him back. Again, he saw nothing.

This is silly, he thought. I don't even know what's happening. The antelope probably ran off when I started down the slide. He raised up again. Still nothing. The grass was so high—it was like a wall around him. He started to get up, then fell back. The only thing keeping him still was fear of ridicule by the mountain man. Francis's orders had been specific: bring back a young buck. Getting up now could ruin it, but if the antelope *had* run off, it was stupid to stay down in the grass all afternoon. He waved the rag again.

That's when the thought hit him: this was all a joke. Mr. Grimes was a great one for jokes. Like sending him down to wave a rag around in a bunch of grass, telling him, of all things, that the antelope would *come* to him. And he'd fallen for it—lock, stock, and barrel. He shook his head. Wouldn't he ever learn?

Again he started to get up, and that's when he saw the antelope. There were two of them. One was quite a bit larger than the other. They were both males, and they had seen Francis move.

Even so, they stood still, absolutely still, not even blinking their eyes.

Francis took in a shallow breath, held it, and leapt to his feet, swinging up his rifle. But as fast as he was, the antelope were faster. In the seeming twitch of two white tails, they were doing close to forty miles an hour, dead away from Francis.

He fired, remembering at the last second to aim at the smaller buck. It wasn't a particularly difficult shot, but Francis was rattled, and he felt certain he'd missed. Yet the young antelope pitched forward and fell.

Francis couldn't believe his eyes. He reloaded at once and walked up to the buck. No second shot was needed; the antelope had been hit in the back of the head, just below the horn base. Francis grabbed him by the horns and began pulling him toward the slide. It was a long haul up, and he was sweating by the time he reached the top where Mr. Grimes was waiting.

"Well, Mr. Tucket. You seem to have done all right down there." The mountain man was grinning, and he fetched a knife from his saddlebag. He made one neat cut down the middle of the dead buck and removed the entrails. He saved the liver and heart and left the rest. "The coyotes will get the leavings. I wasn't sure how you'd do. You can tell a lot about a man when he's hunting antelope. It's the waiting. A lot of 'em get nervous and start fidgeting around. I've known grown men to actually stand up and scare 'em away."

Francis blushed again. "Well," he began, "I can see how something like that could happen. I mean, I almost . . ."

"Generally speaking, though," the mountain man went on as though he hadn't heard, "if a man makes it through once, you don't have to worry about him. He'll pull his load when the time comes, and that's all you can ask of any man."

"I *was* a little nervous," Francis said quietly.

"Well, it didn't hurt your shooting a lot," Mr. Grimes said, pointing toward the antelope's head. "I'd call that a right smart shot."

"I thought I'd missed."

Mr. Grimes nodded. "That happens sometimes. You never know till the smoke clears." There was something about his voice; he seemed to be talking around something. Francis caught it but didn't say anything. By that time Mr. Grimes had a small, smokeless fire going and had spitted the liver.

They ate it when its edge was just turning brown, cutting it in thin strips with Mr. Grimes's knife. Francis thought he had never tasted anything so rich and delicious.

After eating the liver, they returned to the camp by the stream and roasted a whole rear quarter of the buck. Then they spent most of the rest of the afternoon and evening cutting off slices and eating them. By dark, they had consumed close to twelve pounds of fresh meat. Mr. Grimes wrapped the rest in the main part of the antelope's skin and put it in one of the mule packs.

"It doesn't really get good for two or three days," he said. "And if it's well wrapped, it'll keep for more than a week."

They doused the fire and turned in early. Mr. Grimes was asleep as soon as his head hit the saddle.

Francis lay for a time thinking. There was something bothering him and it took him almost five minutes to realize what it was. Then he got up, quietly, and fished one of his rifle balls out of his "possibles" sack. He found the antelope's head where Mr. Grimes had left it, and in the moonless dark he turned it over and put the ball in the hole in the back of the head.

As he suspected, it was much too large a hole to have been made by his rifle. He dropped the head and returned to his bed. From now on, he thought, if that man says up is down and day is night, I'll believe him. Anybody who can make a shot like that, timing it to go off at the same time as another rifle, and hit a running antelope at two—no, three hundred yards, *can't* be wrong.

It was a comforting thought. Francis went to sleep smiling.

—— Chapter Twelve ——

FOR A WEEK they rode at an easy pace, saving the horses. Still they made close to a hundred miles before Mr. Grimes pulled up on the seventh evening.

"How do you feel about a little night riding, Mr. Tucket?" he asked.

"All right," Francis answered. "Why?"

"I sort of figured we could make Spot Johnnie's before turning in. Be nice to have a decent meal and sleep loose for a change."

Francis had no idea what he was talking about.

Not once had he mentioned this Spot Johnnie, but Francis decided not to question the mountain man.

"And we can grain the horses. Especially that mare of yours."

So they rode on. There was half a moon to furnish some light and sometime toward midnight Mr. Grimes pointed down at a light in a shallow valley.

"Spot Johnnie's," he said. "Now when we go in, you stay right out to the side of me—so's it doesn't look like you're sneaking. Okay?"

Francis nodded. They started down, angled across a flat meadow, and approached three log buildings. When they were still a hundred feet from the cabins, Mr. Grimes stopped.

"Ease that hammer down with your thumb, Spot," he said in a voice so low it was almost a whisper. "It's Jason Grimes."

Francis hadn't seen or heard a thing, so it was to his utter and complete surprise that the figure of a man arose suddenly beside him—not five feet away. He jumped.

"Dang it all, Jason," the man said, laughing and shaking his head. "You sure do ruin a man's fun. I was planning to let you get all the way up to the building, and then take that pretty hat of yours off, feather and all."

"That's why I stopped," Mr. Grimes answered.

"Got me a friend here who doesn't understand that kind of fun. He might just put a ball in your gizzard by mistake."

Rather than stop to talk, they kept on riding slowly, and Spot Johnnie walked between them. They pulled up at the front cabin. Light was leaking out around the hide windows, and in its glow, Francis got his first look at Spot Johnnie as Mr. Grimes introduced them. There wasn't really much to see. He could have been fifty or a hundred. He had a gray beard and long hair that hung well past his shoulders, and he wore beaded buckskins. There was no hat on his head; instead he wore a beaded headband to keep his hair out of his eyes. His rifle was a Hawkens. Francis liked him at once—there was a nice sound in his speech, a sort of easy confidence, and his eyes looked merry all the time.

"Figured you were always pretty much of a loner, Jason," Spot said, eyeing Francis. "How'd you come by picking up a cub?"

While Mr. Grimes explained about Francis, a boy of perhaps ten years of age came out of the cabin and took the horses around back. Then the three of them went inside.

At first, the inside of the cabin made Francis homesick. It was all so warm and cheerful. Two children were playing on the floor beneath a huge wooden table. There was a fire in the fireplace, although it wasn't at all cold. On one side of the cabin there were beds, arranged in bunk fashion, and all around the walls hung blankets and jackets and old moccasins. It looked like a home. And then, suddenly, he wasn't so homesick anymore—leaning over a big kettle near the fireplace was a large Indian woman.

It startled him to see the woman, not in a lodge, but in a house. She must be Johnnie's wife, he knew, but he caught himself staring just the same. She made him think of the Pawnee village.

As if reading his mind, Spot Johnnie suddenly spoke up. "And this is my family, Mr. Tucket. That's my wife, Bird Dance, over by the fire, and under the table are Jared and John, and the boy you saw outside was Clarence."

The boys under the table didn't look out. But Bird Dance turned from the fire, smiled, and said in perfect English, "How do you do. I'm sure you must be hungry after riding all day. Please sit down and have some stew and biscuits."

Francis managed to hide his surprise. He smiled —he liked her at once—and turned to the table. Mr. Grimes was already sitting there with Spot.

"How've you been making out, Spot?" Mr. Grimes asked.

"Fit," came the answer. "Pure fit and prime. Got me a full warehouse of furs and a wagon or two due next week from St. Louis to pick 'em up. Been a good year, and it might be a better one next. And you?"

"So-so," Mr. Grimes answered. "Found me a new hole last winter that I figure on trying before snow comes. What you giving for near-prime pelts this year, Spot?"

"You mean in money or trade?"

"Money."

"Two dollars—if it's a big one."

"Seems kinda low . . ."

"I might go three, if I knew the trapper and knew he wasn't out just to give me his culls."

"Fair enough. You got yourself a deal. Now, about provisions. You got everything?"

"All but sugar. It's running three dollars a pint —*wholesale*. So I've put off ordering it, hoping it would go down a mite."

"Fine. We'll need the usual. Your oldest boy can put it together tomorrow. In the meantime, I've got some questions that need answering."

They had to stop talking to eat the stew and biscuits, which proved to be worth at least a ten-day ride. Francis ate four bowls of stew and half a dozen fresh biscuits before Bird Dance cleared the table.

"Now," Spot said, lighting a pipe and propping his legs on a small three-legged stool. "What kind of questions you got, Jason?"

"About Indians, Spot. There's something downright funny going on and I can't pin it down. Take Braid, for instance—"

"*You* take him," Spot cut in. "I've had enough of that skunk to hold me for all my days."

"What happened?"

"Nothing—to me. But Braid's thinking of taking over the whole Pawnee nation, way it looks, and for nothing but war. He was here a while back asking for things—powder, mostly, and caps. Only he didn't ask for 'em the way a man might. He said, 'The *Pawnee* want powder and the *Pawnee* want caps,' just like he was talking for the whole tribe. I don't like it."

"I thought he was getting a little feisty," Mr. Grimes said.

"It's not just things like taking this boy," Spot said, gesturing toward Francis. "That's bad enough. But Braid's also been raiding. There've been two wagon trains through here, and they both lost some people to Pawnees being led by Braid."

"Those two trains," Francis said, interrupting, "did any of the people in them mention losing a little girl?"

Spot scratched his head. "No . . . mostly they didn't want to talk about those they'd lost, so they didn't talk about the Indians much at all. One woman—I think it was a brown-haired woman—asked me if the Indians always killed captives. She was pretty broken up about losing a boy—"

"I'm that boy," Francis said. "She's my mother." He sighed. Then at least his mother was alive, and most likely his father. "She didn't mention a girl named Rebecca?"

"Nope—at least not that I recollect. But as I said, the people mostly didn't talk about the raid."

They were silent for a while, thinking. Francis was imagining the muscled figure of Braid nestled just over his rifle's sights.

"Braid's stupid," Spot continued after a minute or two. "He's talking about making a clean sweep, or so I hear, and driving all whites from Pawnee territory."

"That's a bit strong," Mr. Grimes said. "He might hit a train or two, but I don't think he'll bother us—I mean you and me. It would only hurt him to put us under—he'd get no more trade."

"All the same," Spot said, "if I were you, and I knew Braid was around somewhere, I'd make sure I had my shoulder blades covered by a tree."

Mr. Grimes shrugged. "I do that anyway—just

natural. But I don't like this other thing much. If there's anything worse than one mad Pawnee, it's a hundred mad Pawnees. Braid's stirring up a war, maybe. Not so good . . ." His voice trailed off.

And that finished any talk for another thirty minutes or so, while they ate and drank *still* more. Francis had thought he was full, but he was fast changing his eating patterns. He was learning that when you *can* eat, you eat. It might be a couple of days before you got a chance to eat again.

"Just one question," Mr. Grimes said around a mouthful of biscuit. "What's the story on the Crows? I spent a week coming across their stomping grounds and didn't see a one. Usually I get shot at at least once."

"I don't know," Spot answered. "But there's been word they found a big herd of buffalo and spent the summer living in back of the herd. I also heard they've broken up a bit—too many war chiefs or something—and that there's a bunch of small bands out, just taking what they can get when they can get it. But you know the Crows: if you see 'em, more'n likely you're going to have to fight 'em." Spot leaned back and sighed. "Enough of that—I think it's time for a game. Or are you scared? I figured you'd probably given up—seeing how bad I whipped you last time."

"*Whipped* me?" snorted Mr. Grimes. "Did you hear that, Mr. Tucket? This old spot-head thinks he whipped me. Waugh! Drag out the plank and we'll see who whips who in this pond."

"Stakes?" Spot asked, laughing.

"One prime pelt—which I haven't got—against three pints of sugar—which you haven't got. Suit you?"

"Why not? I can always use another pelt."

"Ho—you sure are the one for talk. Where's that plank?"

Spot turned and fetched a flat board from the wall. The board was about two feet long, and at either end a heavy leather thong was lashed. Francis could make neither head nor tail of it, even when Spot put the board down in front of Mr. Grimes and seated himself opposite. The children had been put to bed, but Spot's wife came over from a stool by the fire. She was smiling, and kept smiling while she took their right arms and placed them on the board. When the arms were in such a position that the back of Mr. Grimes's hand was against the back of Spot's, she brought the leather thongs up and around and lashed their elbows in place. Now their arms could move neither forward nor backward, nor up at the elbow.

The two men, with their hands still back-to-back, hooked thumbs. Mr. Grimes looked at Spot, Spot returned the look, they both nodded, and the woman said, "Go!"

It didn't seem to be much of a match at first. The object of the contest was to twist your arm and drag your opponent's thumb down to the board by twisting *his* arm. At the start, Spot got the jump. Mr. Grimes didn't stop him until his thumb was almost mashed into the board, and then only by an effort that made all the cords in his neck stand out.

They hung like that for a long time, grinning at each other, their breath coming in rasps. Then, ever so slowly, Mr. Grimes started to push Spot's thumb back up. The thumbs stopped again when they were straight up, swung back and forth for a period of ten seconds, then suddenly plunged down until Spot's thumb touched the board.

"Ahh!" he said. "Where'd you get all *that*?"

"Been practicing," Mr. Grimes answered. "Figuring the way you whipped me last time . . ."

"Ha! Woman?" Spot called. "Fetch this badger three pints of brown sugar—not that he earned it, understand, but a deal is a deal."

"Seems there's a snake around here somewhere," Mr. Grimes said, grinning. "I thought you didn't have any sugar?"

"Nope—said I didn't *order* any," Spot answered.

"Lots of difference. Besides, you trying to tell me you don't have a single pelt out there in your pack somewheres?"

"Nope—got *three* I saved from last year."

Francis stared at them. The betting didn't make any sense. They both bet something they said they didn't have, but which they really did have. He was going to ask about it, but just then Mr. Grimes suggested getting some sleep and Francis, who had been sitting with the warm glow of the fire on his back and an extremely full stomach, realized that if he so much as blinked, he would be asleep.

He staggered to the warm corner by the fire, where Spot told him to go, and was soon dead to the world.

— Chapter Thirteen —

MR. GRIMES AND FRANCIS stayed with Spot Johnnie for three days. They had meant to leave sooner, but things kept happening. First there was a joke shooting match between Mr. Grimes and Spot —a joke match because neither of them really tried to win. All they did was trick shooting; kind of show-off stuff, Francis thought. Like Spot throwing a piece of mud in the air, then stooping to pick up his rifle and shooting the mud before it hit the ground. And Mr. Grimes shooting a big rock over five hundred yards away, hitting it three times in a row.

Then the shooting match led to a wrestling match, and the wrestling match led to a giant dinner and warm sun to lie around in and a swim down in the creek by the stable, and before Francis really thought about it at all, three days had disappeared. On the morning of the fourth day, they rose early, packed the mules, and started out.

They were about half a mile from the buildings when they saw the wagons. Mr. Grimes saw them first, as usual.

"Farmers, Mr. Tucket," he said, pointing back past Spot Johnnie's place. Two wagons were visible coming down into the valley, crawling along. They were a good three miles away, but Francis could make out the men walking alongside the oxen. "It could be your chance—if they're going to Oregon. Most likely they are."

Francis didn't understand at first. He wasn't really thinking of himself in connection with wagons. And when he finally caught the mountain man's meaning, somehow it made him feel sad. Still, he nodded. "I guess so—that is, if they wouldn't mind taking a boy along."

"I think they'd probably be happy to have that extra gun," Mr. Grimes said, "especially if Braid's going to do some kicking up."

There was a long moment. The morning sun

caught the mare's mane and made it look almost blue. And how would you like to slow down to ten miles a day, little mare? Francis found himself thinking. How would you like to eat oxen dust and be tied with other horses at night? He looked again at the wagons. There were five showing now—five plodding wagons settled into the ruts across the prairie.

And he didn't want to be with them; not with the dust and the slow wagons and all the people carrying punch bowls. There was more to it now—more than if he were just another train boy. He knew more. He knew Indians, and how to shoot, and how to wrestle—

"You sure do seem to be in powerful thought, Mr. Tucket," Mr. Grimes cut in. "A man would think you're having trouble making up your mind . . ."

There was that, too, Francis thought. How can I just keep going with the mountain man? Mr. Grimes has his own way of life. It's a wild and exciting life, but is it the kind of life for me—for the rest of my life?

Francis shook his head in bewilderment. Then, slowly, he turned toward the wagons.

"Of course"—Mr. Grimes stopped him—"you've got to figure those people are maybe pretty dumb. They won't make Oregon anyways—at least not *this* winter. Here it is early fall, and they're only this far. Way I figure it, they'll be spending winter about halfway there—somewhere in the west part of Dakota Country, where it gets cold."

Francis looked at him. Was the mountain man telling him to stay? Or was he just ridiculing the "farmers" for being dumb?

"Now me," Mr. Grimes continued, his face still blank, "I figure on spending my winter not far from here—where the snow won't get *too* much higher'n a horse and I don't have to worry about much except a few stray Crows. If I get lucky and fill out on beaver fast, I just might come down here and spend the winter with Spot."

"Are you trying to tell me that I'd be better off staying with you through the winter than I would be if I joined that particular wagon train?"

"No-ah, Mr. Tucket, that isn't quite right. I'm not trying to tell you anything. It's your mind, you make it up . . ."

Francis nodded.

". . . but I'd hate to think I plucked you from Braid just so's you could turn out dumb."

Francis felt warm all over—warmer than the morning sun could have made him feel. He hefted his rifle, turned the little mare once more and almost—but not quite—laughed in relief. The truth was he didn't want to leave and it had been handled for him.

Mr. Grimes clucked at the sorrel and moved ahead. He didn't look back—not at the wagons or at Francis. He rode straight, his derby and feather aimed dead ahead.

Francis caught up. He didn't look back at the train either. It might as well not have been there. He felt that he should thank the mountain man, but what could he say? A straight "thank you" would probably only make him snort.

"The way I figured it, Mr. Grimes," he said finally, his eyes straight ahead, "if a guy's gotta spend a winter, he might as well spend it the best way he can . . ."

The mountain man smiled.

— Chapter Fourteen —

TWO DAYS AWAY from Spot Johnnie's, Mr. Grimes stopped on the edge of a deep canyon.

"From here on, Mr. Tucket, we'll see no more people—Indians or otherwise."

Francis nodded, and believed him. They wound down a narrow trail to the bottom of the canyon. It was a dark place, with sheer walls and a thick forested floor, and in the bottom was a narrow stream. Mr. Grimes put his sorrel in the middle of this, and instructed Francis to do the same with his mare.

"We go up it awhile," he said, "and that's how we make *sure* we don't see any people."

That "awhile" proved to be two days long. When they camped at night, Mr. Grimes didn't allow a fire. And in the mornings, when they got ready to leave, he went around brushing out signs of their horses and making the campsite look as though they'd never been there.

At the end of the second day, they moved away from the stream. The canyon had widened into a valley more than ten miles across, and Mr. Grimes headed toward the right—or northern—edge. The forest was much thicker, the ground softer, but still he allowed no traces of their presence to remain at any campsite. His sharp eyes missed nothing, and he left no trail. Where the horses' hooves sank into the ground, he painstakingly pushed sticks under the depressions to raise them. When a twig was broken, he rubbed dirt on the broken end to make it look old.

"It's still pretty plain," he explained to Francis, standing over a hoof mark that Francis couldn't see even though he knew where it lay. "But in a couple of days, the best Kiowa tracker in the world couldn't find us—and neither will another trapper."

"Why are you being so careful?" Francis asked. He was tired of going slow.

"You heard the reasons just now, Mr. Tucket. One is the trappers. It's not that I'm greedy, at least no more than the next. But there's just enough beaver where we're headed to keep a man going, so long as he doesn't clean 'em out in one season. I wouldn't clean 'em out—and neither would another *good* trapper . . ."

"Then what are you worried about?"

"Every man who traps beaver isn't all that thoughtful. We come up here and take out a catch, and if somebody follows us who doesn't think about next season, he might clean out the beaver—lock, stock, and prime pelt. So I'm careful. I'm not worried, Mr. Tucket, just careful."

"All right, that's one reason. What's the other?"

"Indians; Crows, to be exact. We're on the edge of their country, and they're kind of unpredictable. We're going to be spread up and down the canyon, traps all over, and if they find out we're up here, they can make it mean for us. So we're careful about them, too. Any *other* questions, Mr. Tucket?"

"No, sir."

When they finally got where they were going— a shallow meadow about three miles wide and ten miles long, leading away from the canyon—Francis could see the reason for caution. Down the middle of the meadow was a long string of beaver ponds, one joined to the next by a short neck of water. Francis knew nothing of beaver, but he guessed there were probably hundreds of them.

Mr. Grimes led the way up the meadow, and it took them one whole day of slow riding to get to the northern end, and the sound of the beaver, slapping their tails against the water, stayed ahead of them all the way.

"Well, Mr. Tucket," the mountain man said, when they finally stopped, "I make it out to be a pretty fair season for us. What say we make a home?"

First they had to build a house, and although it wasn't much more than a large lean-to, it seemed like a house by the time the roof was finally finished. Mr. Grimes gave Francis an ax from one of the mule packs, and he cut all the poles for the lean-to while the mountain man did what he called the "count" on the beaver stream. It took Francis the better part of a week to cut enough long timbers for the walls and roof, and during that time, he saw Mr. Grimes only in the evenings and early mornings.

At first it didn't bother him. There was a job to be done, and Francis, with his two good arms, was better equipped to do it. But by the fourth day he felt irritated because it seemed to him that the mountain man was just taking a vacation while he put up the house. Over morning coffee, he said, "What are you doing out there all day? Not that I really care, understand. But a guy has to learn—"

Mr. Grimes snorted and then sipped his coffee. "Seems to me you *ought* to care. I mean, I'm out there just resting on my stomach along the creek while you slave away on our castle. *I'd* care. But if I tell you, will you promise not to laugh?"

"Sure."

"I'm counting the grown beaver in each pond, one at a time."

Francis didn't laugh, because he didn't understand. "Why are you counting them?" he asked.

"So when we start taking 'em, we'll know how many we can take out of each pond without ruining it. Of course, trapping all the beaver in the world won't help us if we don't have a house to dry the pelts in . . ."

Francis didn't ask any more questions. Instead he got the house up, back in the trees along the meadow, and Mr. Grimes finished his count just in time to help with the last poles on the roof. Then they put up a small pole corral for the horses and mules, and when that was finished, they moved in. Now, Mr. Grimes explained, there was nothing to do but wait.

"It's like this, Mr. Tucket," he said. "There are

two times to trap beaver. In late fall and early spring. In the fall, you catch them when their coats are turning prime—getting ready for the cold. In the spring, you catch them before they lose their winter pelts. Now I prefer to catch them in the fall —and I'll let you guess why."

Francis thought for a minute, then shrugged. "I don't know. Is the market better?"

"True, but that's not really why. If you take a mother beaver in the spring, you might take her just after she's had young. You not only trap the mother, but kill the young because you take away their milk. If I take her in the fall, her babies—the kits—haven't even started yet and I only kill one beaver—"

"But what's the difference?" Francis interrupted. "I mean, she's still gone, and she still can't have the kits."

"Right. But beaver mate up in the fall, and they mate for life. If I trap a female in the fall, the male that would have mated with her goes on and finds another. It all works out, Mr. Tucket, it all works out."

Francis thought about it, nodded, then asked, "When do we get started?"

"About two weeks after the first cold snap, when their pelts firm up. I figure down here, in the bottom of this canyon, we ought to see some cold before long."

It was true, Francis knew. Most of the aspens had taken on a golden hue, and the scrub oaks were already losing some leaves. The days were still warm but the nights had a way of turning cold, and moving out in the morning from beneath the warm buffalo robe Mr. Grimes had given him got harder each day. Also, the fact that there was little to do made it hard to get up.

Francis found you either had too much to do, or nothing. When there was nothing, his thoughts turned always to his mother and father, and he wondered how they were doing in Oregon. He missed them, but for some strange reason, he missed Rebecca more. She had always been sort of a nuisance to him, following him when he wanted to be alone, asking him dumb questions—this made him smile when he thought of some of the questions he asked Mr. Grimes—and yet he missed her.

Finally the cold weather came. One morning, Francis crawled out of his buffalo robe and the world was a land of crisp whiteness. Frost covered everything. Mr. Grimes was already up, humming —of all things—while he sharpened his skinning and fleshing knife.

"To work, Mr. Tucket," he announced. "Our holiday's over."

Now they had just two weeks to cut enough bait sticks—short pieces of green aspen—store them along the stream, plan the trap line, make skin-drying hoops of the same green aspen, and sort and "purify" the traps.

And with all this work to be done, company arrived. Francis, for a change, saw them first, but only because Mr. Grimes was out cutting bait sticks. Francis was in front of the hut, lashing some drying hoops together with thongs of fresh rawhide from a deer that had wandered into their camp. Across the meadow came four horses. Two of them were being led, and two of them were being ridden. They were quite far away, too far to identify the riders as anything but men, too far away to allow any wild guessing. But even so, Francis made a wild guess and decided they were Crows.

All of this took just five seconds. On the sixth second, he was in the house, looking out through an opening in its side. His cheek lay against the stock of his rifle, the hammer was back, a percussion cap covered the nipple, the barrel was charged, and his finger was on the trigger.

The two men rode, as though drawn by an invisible cord, straight toward the cabin.

Chapter Fifteen

WHEN THE MEN and horses were still some two hundred yards away, they stopped. One man dismounted and studied the soft ground of the meadow. He turned and said something to the man who was still mounted, and then swung back into his saddle. From the way he dismounted and mounted and the way they rode, Francis now realized that they weren't Indians. More than likely, especially since they had pack horses, they were trappers.

He eased up from the rifle, but only a little.

They could still be up to no good, and it didn't hurt to be ready. He watched for some sign of their intentions—and got it when they were just a hundred yards from the house.

One of them slipped his rifle from its buckskin case and laid the gun across his lap. The other then did the same, and Francis could feel the hair on his neck rise. Nobody dropping in for a friendly visit would make a point of coming armed and ready.

His cheek went back to the stock of his rifle. He wanted to run out back and get the mountain man, but he didn't know how far he'd have to go. And if he left the pack mules and all their equipment alone, even for a minute, everything might be gone by the time they got back.

No, he couldn't leave. There was nothing else to do—he would simply have to stay and try to bluff them out.

Approximately thirty yards from the house, the two men stopped. They were about twenty feet apart, sitting their horses loosely, but both of their rifles were aimed in the general direction of the lean-to. Francis could make out their features easily. One of them was rather short and bearded. The other was lean, also bearded, fairly tall, and it was he who leaned forward in the saddle and called:

"Yo, the house! Anybody home?"

Francis said nothing. He watched.

"Up there! The house!" the man called again. "Anybody home?"

They were getting uneasy. Francis could tell by the way the lean one angled his rifle upward as he talked. Even at that range, the muzzle looked like a cave. Might as well say something, he thought, before they just fire away.

"Who are you, and what do you want?" he called, trying to make his voice sound gruff and older.

"Name's Bridger," answered the lean one. "Jim —to people who come into the light. This here's my partner, Jake Barnes. And all we want is a little hospitality."

Sure, thought Francis—you're Jim Bridger and I'm Kit Carson. If you really are Jim Bridger, you sure wouldn't just amble blind into a trap like this. How do you know I'm not an Indian? You could have been following anybody's tracks.

"You lost your tongue in there?" the lean one yelled again. "I said that the name's Bridger . . ."

"I heard you," Francis answered. The man was lying. He was sure of it. He brought up the front sight of his rifle. It made him feel funny, aiming at a man. But he'd been caught off guard once—by Braid—and it wasn't going to happen twice. "I'm not sure I believe it. Can you prove you're Jim Bridger?"

"*Prove?* What's to prove? I'm just sitting here, ain't I? I said I was Bridger, didn't I? What more do you need?"

There it was. He said he was Bridger, but Francis was positive he was lying, and so they were stalemated. There was nothing to do but wait for Mr. Grimes.

"If you're *really* Jim Bridger," Francis called, "you won't mind just sitting there for a while—"

"What for?"

"Until—until somebody comes who can tell me if that's the truth."

"And what if I decide to ride off? Or come plowing *at* you?"

"I've got a gun on you."

"I figured *that.*"

"I'll use it."

"Maybe. When's this man coming?"

"Soon."

"What's his name?"

"You don't need to know."

"All right. I'll wait for a spell. But if he doesn't come soon, and I mean *soon*, you better figure on using that gun."

The minutes dragged. The sun got hotter, and flies began buzzing around the horses.

He had no idea how long Mr. Grimes would be gone, Francis realized. Somehow, half an hour crawled past. It was the longest half hour of his life. And Bridger—or the man who said he was Bridger —didn't help any. If he had gotten nervous, or started to move around, Francis would have felt better. But he didn't. He just sat his horse—cool, calm, waiting. And the smaller man did the same.

Forty minutes passed, fifty, then an hour was gone. And that was enough.

The lean one moved. He straightened in his saddle and called. "Time's up. I haven't got ten years to waste. Now I'm gonna turn around and ride out of here. My partner's coming with me. I don't think you'll touch anything off—but if you do, you'll get only one of us. And the other one will get you, just as sure as winter's coming."

This was it then; the test. Francis reset his sight. It would be suicide to let the man go. He and his partner might ride off a mile, turn around, and sneak back to kill them at night.

Even as the lean one turned his horse, and the partner followed suit, Francis knew he couldn't do it. It was one thing to shoot somebody who was attacking you, but to just come out and shoot a man because you thought he might be lying—

"Jim Bridger!" the voice was loud, cutting through Francis's thoughts. It came from the side of the clearing he couldn't see, but he knew that voice. It belonged to Jason Grimes. "You figuring on riding out of here without taking a cup of coffee with an old friend?"

The two men stopped their horses. "I figured you was up here somewhere," the lean one said. "And to be downright truthful about it all, I *did* stop for some coffee. I figured old Jason Grimes was as good as the next for a free spot of java. But before you get all relaxed about us stopping for a while, maybe you ought to know there's a two-legged terror in that shack over there with a gun on us. Shouldn't we ask *him* about stopping?"

"What . . . ?" Mr. Grimes turned to the building. "Oh . . . how long you been here?"

"Seems like ten years," Jake Barnes said. "Maybe an hour, really."

"And Mr. Tucket kept you at bay all that time?"

"Who?" Jim Bridger asked.

"Mr. Tucket." Mr. Grimes turned again to the building. "Mr. Tucket, come on out here and meet the men you've been holding."

So it *was* Bridger. Francis felt like an idiot. Still,

he couldn't stay out of sight forever. He stepped out of the doorway and walked toward the horses.

"Why, it's ain't nothing but a cub." Jim Bridger snorted. "Jake, we've been sitting here worried about a *cub.*"

That broke the ice, and the two men dismounted, grinning at Francis.

"Where'd you get him?" Bridger asked.

While Francis made a fire, Mr. Grimes told the two mountain men about him. By the time the explanation was finished, the coffee was ready, and they all sipped it and chewed on venison. After that, the men smoked and Francis sat quietly thinking. There was something bothering him. Finally he could hold it no longer.

"Mr. Bridger," he asked, "how did you find us?"

"Why, we just followed your trail, boy. Easy as following a herd of buffalo. But don't worry. We covered tracks coming in—ours *and* yours."

Francis looked at Mr. Grimes. He was smiling.

"Ho!" he exclaimed. "You're feeding Mr. Tucket a nettle. Bad for his liver. The fact is, Mr. Tucket, there's another meadow like this up a ways that belongs to Mr. Bridger. I found this one last year about the same time he found his. We met coming out, so he knew I'd be here about now. Unless I miss my guess, he's on his way up there now."

Bridger nodded. "Caught, cold turkey. Boy, never lie in front of Jason Grimes. You'll lose every time. Say"—he turned to Mr. Grimes—"how are you and Braid getting on lately?"

That triggered off another round of talk. They covered the Indian tribes—Pawnee, Sioux, and finally, while Francis made another pot of coffee, the Crow.

"You might be extra careful when you go out," Bridger told Mr. Grimes. "We saw some fresh Crow sign down at the mouth of the valley. Whole tribe—man, woman, child, and dog. Looking for a wintering ground, I reckon, so they probably won't bother you. But I don't think they'd pass up a chance at those rifles if they ran across you."

Mr. Grimes nodded. "The Crows and the weather—you can't tell about either one. But I think I'd take a blizzard to a Crow any day . . ."

Francis listened to them intently. His stomach was full of warm coffee and jerky, evening was coming down, the fire felt good, and he was in the company of a living legend—Jim Bridger. What more could he ask? Why think about such unpleasant things as snowstorms or Indians at a time like this? Better just to listen, because someday he would want to tell his family everything about this meeting with the fabulous Jim Bridger.

—— Chapter Sixteen ——

BRIDGER AND HIS PARTNER pulled out early the following morning. Before they were even out of sight, Mr. Grimes said, "Back to work. We lost a good part of a day, Mr. Tucket, and we couldn't afford it."

He walked out of camp to get more bait sticks, and Francis went back to work on the drying hoops.

Actually, they were fairly simple to make. He took a slim piece of springy willow or aspen, eight feet long, and bent it into a circle about three feet across. Then he lashed the ends together with wet, green rawhide that seemed to shrink when it dried and made the two ends of the willow become one piece. After a beaver was skinned, the hide was put in this hoop and with lacing around the sides pulled toward the edges so that when it was dry it would be a hard plate of hide with fur on one side.

Mr. Grimes wanted two hundred of these hoops. Francis ran out of rawhide that evening on the fiftieth hoop. He told Mr. Grimes about it.

"Well, Mr. Tucket, the woods are full of deer and you've got a rifle. Seems like a fairly simple problem to me . . ."

So the next morning Francis walked quietly through the pine glades, glad of a chance to get away from the lean-to. Not three hundred yards from the house, he stopped on the edge of a small clearing, just to enjoy the morning, and found himself facing a nice three-point buck.

There was the deer, and there was Francis, with perhaps fifty feet between them. He raised his rifle, aimed at the buck's shoulder, and squeezed the trigger. The little Lancaster cracked sharply—higher and faster sounding than Mr. Grimes's big bull gun —and the deer took two steps forward, sagging as he walked, and fell. Francis reloaded, as cool as though he were shooting buffalo chips, and aimed at the deer's head. He fired again and it was over.

He started forward, then, remembering what he'd been taught, stopped and reloaded again.

And he suddenly started shaking all over, as though he had a chill. He couldn't even walk right and had to sit down. It was silly, but he was nervous about the deer—nervous and rattled. He didn't know what it was—he just had to sit down for a minute.

When he got up, it was as though it had never happened. He grabbed the deer by its rack and dragged it back to camp. There he skinned it and cut the wet hide into strips half an inch wide. By late afternoon, he was again making hoops, the incident all but forgotten.

Mr. Grimes came in at about four o'clock, his arm full of sticks, and Francis told him about the deer.

"Buck fever, Mr. Tucket—or, as some call it, gun jaw. Most people get it the first time they think about shooting anything bigger than a rabbit. Usually it only hits a man once or twice—and then only if he's had time to think about it. You're lucky."

"Why?"

" 'Cause some get it *before* they shoot. They can't even pull the trigger. I watched one man—and this is pure gospel—stand up against a bear that didn't like him at all, and all he did was aim his rifle and say, 'Bang.'"

"You mean he didn't shoot?"

"Nope. Didn't even draw his hammer. If I hadn't been there to kill the bear, that man would have been nothing in a second or two. Unless the bear could understand English. Hah!"

But Francis couldn't laugh at the joke. He remembered shaking all over, and he hoped that when the time came—*if* it came—for him to face something dangerous, he wouldn't do something dumb like saying "Bang."

By the end of the week the hoops were finished, and Mr. Grimes had gathered all the bait sticks. Next came the traps. There were fifty of them—big, double-springed traps with bait-pan trips. They all had to be smoked over a low fire of green aspen to take away the smell of man. So Francis was put in charge of the smoking fire, working ten traps at a time. They were hung over the fire with a long pole and taken off with a forked stick. Once smoked, they could not be touched by human hands.

After the traps were smoked, they were hung three to a stick, so that Mr. Grimes could carry them to the individual ponds without touching them.

About halfway through the second week of

working, as if on demand, cold settled in and held for a few hours. The next morning, Mr. Grimes reported that they'd start trapping that day.

"There'll be ice on the ponds," he said. "That makes it easier. The beaver sort of give themselves away by cutting holes in the ice. All you have to do is drop a trap in the hole and wait. They come right into it. Even if the ice melts off—and it probably will before the day is out—they still use the same place. Sort of like you'd use a hallway in a house."

While he talked, he was working, lashing bait sticks and trap sticks to a long aspen pole. This pole, with twenty-one traps, he handed to Francis. Then he made another one, just like the first.

They rode out toward the first pond well before noon. Francis was almost excited. All this labor, and now he would actually see what they'd been working toward. And, he thought, just maybe, the back-breaking labor would slack off a bit.

They dismounted at the first pond, and sure enough, despite the fact that it was turning out to be a fairly warm day, the pond was covered by a thin layer of ice. At one point, near the dam of sticks and mud along the bank, there was a broken, jagged hole about two feet across. In this hole the mountain man placed one trap, set, on a pole that angled down into the water and stuck in the mud on the bottom. The trap was well under water and above the trap he tied several bait sticks to the pole with rawhide.

"But won't the beaver see the trap?" Francis asked.

"He'll see it, all right," came the answer, gruff and short. "But he won't take *notice*, Mr. Tucket. At least not till he steps in the trap. Old Daddy Beaver goes more by his nose than his eyes, and if you smoked these traps right, he'll think that piece of iron is another hunk of wood."

So it went, pond by pond. It was nearly dark when they finished the fourteenth pond. Francis had done nothing but hand out traps and bait sticks, and yet he was exhausted—and more than ready to head back for the house and a warm fire.

Mr. Grimes headed back to the first pond.

"They're good enough to let us trap 'em, Mr. Tucket," he said. "The least we can do is keep up."

"You mean there'll be one trapped already?" Francis asked.

"More than one, or I miss my guess."

And of course, he was right. The first pond yielded one, same with the second, nothing in the third, one in the fourth and so on. By midnight or so, with Francis all but falling off his mare, they had eleven prime beaver.

Mr. Grimes had reset all the traps, and although he didn't say anything, Francis was living in a quiet horror that they might start all over again, and *again*, and just keep going until they had two hundred beaver.

But the trapper headed his sorrel back to camp. Once there, after the fire was going and coffee started, he went to work skinning the beaver. And Francis, who could think of nothing but crawling into his big buffalo robe and forgetting everything, was told to stay up and stretch the hides on the hoops.

By eight in the morning—with no sleep—they had finished the twenty-six beaver they had trapped.

"We sleep till noon, Mr. Tucket," the mountain man announced. "Then we start over. And we've got more work now, because after this haul, we'll have to move the traps."

Francis didn't hear the last words about more work. He was asleep.

At noon he didn't want to get up. He wouldn't have wanted to rise with fifteen hours of sleep, but with just four, he almost *couldn't* get up. Mr. Grimes dumped cold water on his face and he did get up, sputtering, and after a little fresh venison, they started again.

Francis lost all track of time. It didn't seem possible to him that human beings could live and work on such an insane schedule. Work at midnight, go to bed at dawn. Get up in four hours and work some more. Ride out with traps and bait sticks, come back with dead, wet beaver. Skin and stretch. Sleep. Eat while you worked, while you rode. Set traps. Close your eyes for what seemed like a second, then open them and work again.

Finally, Mr. Grimes stopped. Five days could have passed, or maybe five years—Francis didn't know. All he knew was that two hundred beaver pelts were hanging and drying inside the house. It was impossible not to know that, for their stench was overpowering.

"We sleep now, Mr. Tucket, as long as we want," the trapper said, grinning. Francis was standing in front of him, almost falling down. "The pelts have to dry for a week at least. I'll wake you at the end of the week."

Oh, no, you won't, Francis thought, grabbing his buffalo robe and heading upwind of the building. Not in a week. I won't even be *started* catching up in a week. Wake me in January sometime, or maybe next spring. Better yet, don't *ever* wake me.

— Chapter Seventeen —

THE WEEK OF IDLE RESTING that Mr. Grimes had promised Francis never took place, but it wasn't the mountain man's fault.

What happened to ruin the week was the sudden arrival of more "company." But this time, the company didn't consist of friends of Jason Grimes. They arrived on the third day after all the pelts had been hung to dry.

Contrary to what he had thought, Francis didn't sleep even for a day. After ten hours of solid snoring, he was up gathering wood. And by the second day, he was practically bored stiff.

"Don't fret on so much, Mr. Tucket," the trapper said when Francis began grumbling. "A man would think you wanted to go back to work. Rest up a mite. There'll be plenty to do."

Francis snorted. "I wouldn't even mind some more trapping. It's better than just sitting around, getting soft."

"Ah, Mr. Tucket, relax. Trap more beaver and you'd just have to sit around for another week. These things take time."

So Francis had dreamed up things to do. He made bullets—when he already had enough to stand off a small army. He took to riding around the meadow along the stream, not going anywhere in particular, just riding.

And he was riding on the morning of the third day, out along the stream, just angling across it, not paying much attention to what he was doing, when something whistled past his cheek, brushing him lightly—almost like a fly. He reached his hand up absently, and at that instant, the horse stepped on a rock and stumbled.

The sudden movement saved Francis's life. The second arrow—which would have hit him squarely in the middle of the chest—whirred past and buried itself in the muck of a beaver dam ten yards upstream.

"Heeah!" Francis screamed, and at the same second fired his rifle in the air. He had two purposes in mind for shooting the rifle. First, it would warn Mr. Grimes. Second, it would get the mare running.

And run she did. Like a little bomb going off beneath Francis, she was out of the stream and at a full gallop in the space of one breath, while he clung to her back like a flea.

She ran straight ahead, and luckily she happened to be pointed toward the camp. But unluckily, she was also pointed toward the Indians, who were hidden in the brush along the stream *between* Francis and the camp, and she took him right through the middle of them.

Francis hadn't seen the Indians, and suddenly he was ten feet away from all five of them. They were five Crows painted for war, ready, and wanting one thing—to make Francis look like a porcupine.

Arrows whistled by him, and Francis felt as though the world had suddenly gone crazy. Painted faces popped up in front of him, screeched, loosed a feathered missile, and disappeared. Somebody fired a gun right by his face, and it deafened him. He felt a hand grab at his leg, and he managed to shake it off. Another hand came up; he clubbed it down with his empty rifle and—he was free!

He was out of the ring of faces and arrows, flying along with the mare.

He looked back. He had seen no horses, but he knew that the Indians wouldn't be too far from their mounts. It was nearly two miles to camp—two long miles. His horse was well fed and with any kind of a lead, he could probably beat them.

He studied the ground ahead. It was smooth, grassy—ideal for running. He looked back again, and saw that two Indians were mounted and starting after him. As he watched, three others burst out of a stand of willows near where they'd jumped Francis.

It would be a chase. Francis studied his lead—a hundred yards, no more. And he was holding an empty rifle. I *have* to beat them, he thought. He had a good mount in his Indian pony, but the Crows were also riding Indian ponies. It stood to reason that out of five ponies, at least one would be as fast or faster than his. He couldn't expect miracles *all* the time.

Sure enough, one of the ponies was as fast as his little mare. But two others were faster, and they gained rapidly. Before he'd covered half a mile, they had cut his hundred-yard lead in half.

Francis leaned forward. "Run! If I ever needed speed, I need it now."

She was full-out already. She put her ears back and stretched an inch or two, but it didn't help much.

Another half mile, he thought, watching the two Indians gaining on him, and they'll be alongside of me. Then what?

Forty yards now, and one of the Indians raised his bow and loosed an arrow.

Francis, looking back, saw the arrow rise in a slow arc and fall toward him. He felt his stomach tighten as his eyes followed its course.

It fell short—by ten yards or so. The Indian fitted another arrow to the bow and aimed.

He's getting the range, Francis thought. Only thirty yards separated them now.

Francis nudged his pony just as the Indian shot his second arrow. The mare veered to the left, still at a dead run, and the arrow missed.

Twenty yards now. They can't miss again, he thought. Not at this short range.

Only fifteen yards, and now two Indians raised their bows.

"No!" Francis cried. "You can't . . ."

Then he heard it. Far off—a noise like the sound of muted thunder. A second later, he heard something whisper over his head, and the lead Indian fell from his horse.

The second Indian veered aside—releasing his arrow at the same time, but missing Francis.

The Hawkens—the great Hawkens of Jason Grimes had done it again.

Francis eased up a bit and looked for the mountain man. It was still almost a quarter of a mile to camp—an impossible range, an impossible shot.

Now Francis saw him—a speck that was leaning against a tree by the camp. At this range it was impossible to tell what the mountain man was doing, but in a moment Francis knew. A cloud of smoke jumped out in front of him, and the sound of a shot followed.

Francis whirled to watch the Indians. One of the ponies somersaulted, throwing his rider heavily.

That still left three. And those three stopped, dismounted, and hid behind the available cover.

Francis dropped down to a canter. It was safe now, and the mare was blowing pretty hard. Even so, it wasn't but a few moments before he was dismounting at the camp.

Mr. Grimes was smiling. "I do declare, Mr. Tucket. You sure pick some mighty funny people to be horse racing with. If you were all *that* hard up for something to do, I might have raced you myself. You didn't have to go and find a bunch of Crows."

"Well, you know how it is," Francis answered, returning the smile, though he was shaking inside and felt a little sick to his stomach. "I was getting pretty bored, just sitting around all the time. A fellow needs *some* action now and then."

"Used to be that way myself, before I lost my arm. Still, I wish you'd come and ask me before you do those things." He pointed at the Indians in the field. One of them had mounted and was heading away at a run. The mountain man shrugged. "No sense doing any more fancy shooting. One of them would be bound to get away."

"Where is he going?" Francis asked.

"For help, Mr. Tucket. And I expect not too far, the way he's riding. Well, you *said* you wanted something to do—some action. Unless I miss my guess, before long you're going to get all the action you ever wanted. Unless . . ."

"Unless what?"

"Unless we run, Mr. Tucket. And stay ahead."

"But we can't run," Francis said. "There are two of them left, watching us. They'd know right where we went."

"I swear, Mr. Tucket, you're getting smarter every day. So it appears that what we've got to do is get rid of those two Indians in the field."

"We?"

"Sure. Were you figuring on doing it all by yourself?"

Francis looked out across the meadow. Two ponies stood grazing almost a mile away. But the Indians weren't in sight. They could be anywhere, everywhere.

"How do we do it?"

"Simple, Mr. Tucket. We just walk out there until they shoot at us, then we shoot back."

Francis suddenly remembered that his rifle was empty. He reloaded it quickly.

"All right, Mr. Tucket, let's go. We don't have all day."

The mountain man started walking out across the meadow, his rifle draped casually across his shoulder. He looked for all the world as though he were just going for a morning stroll, or perhaps to hunt rabbits.

Except these rabbits, Francis thought, hurrying to catch up, aren't like normal rabbits. These rabbits shoot back.

— Chapter Eighteen —

FRANCIS WOULD NEVER FORGET that morning "walk." He was afraid, and as they walked closer to where he thought the two Indians were, he became more and *more* afraid. His forehead ran with sweat, and it was all he could do to keep from stopping, or turning, or yelling. But he didn't, he couldn't, because the mountain man was really depending on him.

"You take the one on the right when they jump us, Mr. Tucket," Mr. Grimes said, in his usual casual voice, as they walked. "I'll do my best on the left one."

So Francis couldn't afford to let fear dominate his actions. If he froze up, or ran, it could mean the death of Mr. Grimes. If he missed, or shot a second late, Mr. Grimes would be gone.

He tried to calm down so he could watch the grass for movement, or see any signs in the soft dirt. But his fear was too real. And then Mr. Grimes stopped, held up his hand, and said, "Mind now, Mr. Tucket. They're close. I can feel 'em."

Francis couldn't feel anything. All he could think was that somehow, some way, they had walked *past* the Indians and he would get an arrow in his back any second.

"Now!"

That's all he heard—that shout from Mr. Grimes. From then on, everything was automatic. In front of them, not ten feet away, two painted faces and bronze chests rose. Two arrows were pulled back on taut strings. Two Indian throats let out a roaring sound.

Francis fired without aiming. He just pointed his rifle in the general direction of the Indian on his right side and pulled the trigger; then he turned and ran.

He ran until he stumbled and fell, and then he

lay on the ground and was sick. Sick from fear, and sick from having fired his rifle at a man, no matter the man's intent.

Mr. Grimes came up to him a moment later.

"Did—did I?"

"Did you shoot him?"

Francis nodded.

"Yes, Mr. Tucket, and a fair shot it was, too. It kept him occupied long enough for me to finish him."

"You mean I didn't—kill—him?"

"Nope. You only winged him. Creased him along the head. But it was enough to give him something else to think about till I could get in close."

Francis sat up. The grass was still cool, but the sun felt good. Better, far better than it had a few moments before. "We did it, eh, Mr. Grimes?"

"No-ah, Mr. Tucket, that isn't quite true. We did *part* of it. We still have to get out of this place before that brave comes back. And the longer you sit there, the more likely it is some brave's gonna wind up with your hair for a dance tonight . . ."

"Aren't you forgetting something?" Francis asked. "One of those Indians was thrown by his pony and that Indian is still around. He'll follow us."

"Not without a horse, he won't. And we're going to have their horses under beaver pelts. Now
quit your jawing."

At a fast trot the mountain man was heading
back toward the camp. Francis followed him. Once
there, Mr. Grimes started on the beaver pelts,
which were still damp, but dry enough to lash into
bundles to be tied across the horses. He told Francis
to mount up and go after the Indian ponies.

It took only a few minutes. His mare still
smelled all right to the Indian ponies, so they didn't
shy away when he approached. But he had one bad
moment, after he had gathered up the four ponies.
While he was walking them back to camp, he rode
past the Indian who had been thrown.

He was sitting on the ground, and if eyes could
kill, Francis would have been dead. The Indian was
trying to draw his bow, but Francis could see that
an injured shoulder wouldn't allow this action. In
addition, one of his legs was twisted under him.
Francis rode past quietly.

Mr. Grimes had been working like a fiend. All
the pelts were lashed into bundles of twenty-five,
stacked and waiting. The mules had been cut loose
and scared off.

"Why don't we use the mules?" Francis asked.

"Too slow," came the quick answer. "And

they'd need grain to move faster. Indian ponies can do it on grass—and we're going to be needing some speed."

That was the last word spoken for over an hour. Working hard, Mr. Grimes and Francis tied the pelts in bundles across the ponies. They were a bit skittish at first—smelling the almost-green hides— but Mr. Grimes kept them tied close to trees until their eyes quit rolling and they stopped blowing.

Then he and Francis mounted their horses and rode out. It had been almost two hours since the brave had gone for help. If the rest of the tribe were within fifteen miles of the camp, the brave and more warriors could be back any second.

Francis and Mr. Grimes rode hard, holding the horses at a steady lope. The Indian ponies kept up easily, and since the temperature had dropped considerably, it was cool enough to allow a decent run without heating the horses too much. South, down the canyon, in the direction they were heading, clouds were building into a gray wall that indicated snow or rain.

Twenty minutes later, back at the cabin, ten Crow braves dismounted and briefly studied the campsite and surrounding area.

They found many things. By feeling the manure

left by the horses and finding it still warm, they knew that Mr. Grimes and Francis had only a short lead. By noting all the beaver traps left behind, they suspected that the two were running in fear.

The leader of the party, an old man—not too old to ride but old enough to have wisdom—smiled at two of the younger men, who were ready to ride their ponies into the ground to catch Mr. Grimes and Francis.

"Let us stay here for a time and help Laughing Pony fix his shoulder and leg, then we will go. We will still have them before daybreak tomorrow."

The young men shook their heads and grumbled but did as he told them to do.

— Chapter Nineteen —

It was almost as if the storm had been waiting for them. Mr. Grimes led, pulling two pack horses and Francis followed pulling two more out into the prairie away from the mouth of the canyon and the snow took on more force, coming so fast that it quickly covered the horses and packs. Francis looked back and could see no trace of any tracks— the snow blew in as fast as they were made—and he smiled.

It was silly to keep going now, when surely their tracks would be blotted by the snow.

Mr. Grimes rode on. To be sure, he eased the pace a bit—impossible not to, the way the wind was driving at them—but he didn't stop.

Another hour passed. The snow was heavier, thicker. It was hard for Francis to see the short ten feet to Mr. Grimes. The temperature had dropped ten or fifteen degrees, and it was now near freezing. Francis took turns with his hands in handling the reins, holding one beneath his shirt to warm while the other got numb on the reins.

And *still* they ran. The world became a mixture of thudding hoofs, howling wind, and slashing snow. Twice, Francis had to force himself to resist cutting loose the two pack horses following him. He had tied their lead lines around his waist, and they kept pulling at him, holding him back, snagging at him.

There was no telling how long Mr. Grimes would have pushed them. He might have tried to ride the storm out. But finally, the little mare decided for them.

One second she was running almost smooth, and the next she was tumbling down under Francis, throwing him clear as she collapsed. He screamed, and luckily Mr. Grimes heard him.

By the time the mountain man had wheeled and stopped, Francis was getting up from the snow. The mare was on her feet, too, but sagging and with her head nearly on the ground. She had run just short of breaking her heart.

Francis loosened the pack horses' lead lines from his waist and looked up, through the snow and wind, at the mountain man, who was still mounted. He could see the verdict on the man's frost-covered face.

"No!" Francis screamed. "I'm not leaving her!"

"Mr. Tucket . . ."

"I'm not leaving her!" Francis repeated. He knew how foolish it sounded. They were out in the open in a violent storm, but he was going to stay with his horse. He didn't care. She hadn't flinched when those five Crows jumped him. *He* wasn't going to leave her to die in a blizzard just for a few beaver pelts.

"Mr. Tucket . . ."

"No!"

Then a strange thing happened. From what Francis knew of Mr. Grimes, he half expected the trapper to go off and leave him alone. Or hit him on the head and carry him.

Mr. Grimes dismounted, hunched his back into the wind, and smiled.

"I do declare, Mr. Tucket, you sure do pick the funniest times to be stubborn. I just hope that when

I get down, you'll be this hot about staying around with me . . ."

Francis realized he was crying. He wasn't sure why. He was tired, but he had won—at least sort of won. There was a lot of snow, and a lot of wind, and he was cold—but it wasn't that kind of crying. He just felt choked. He turned away.

"And now, Mr. Tucket, if we're ever going to see what the world is like *after* this humdinger, we'd better get to work. Help me get these horses around."

Mr. Grimes put all the horses, nose-to-tail, in a tight circle. Then he cut the beaver pelts loose from the Indian ponies and put the packs in the middle of the circle of horses.

"Now hobble 'em," he said, tying a piece of lead rope around one of the ponies' front ankles. "Hobble 'em tight."

Francis worked fast. In no time, all the horses, including his own, were hobbled tight—front and rear.

Then Mr. Grimes went around the circle on the outside and began pushing the horses over, toward the center. When he was done, all of them were lying on their sides, with their backs leaving only a small circle of empty space around the beaver pelts. Mr. Grimes went around and pulled all the horses' front and back legs together and hog-tied them. Now they couldn't get up, no matter how hard they tried.

"And now, Mr. Tucket, why don't you and me catch up on a little sleep?"

Stepping over the horses to the center, he motioned Francis to do the same. They cleared off the snow in a little empty space, and began covering it with beaver pelts cut loose from the packs.

They used almost half of the two hundred near-dry pelts, fur-side up, and when they'd finished, the circle of space was completely covered with warm fur. They lay down and covered themselves with the remaining pelts.

It was a cozy, warm place. The horses' backs gave off heat and stifled the sound of the wind. Francis was almost asleep as he put the last pelt in place. In a few seconds, just as he was drifting off, he heard the hoarse snore of the mountain man next to him.

—— Chapter Twenty ——

FRANCIS DIDN'T KNOW for sure how long they slept in their horseflesh shelter. Perhaps ten hours. Then they lay awake for a time, not talking, just listening to the wind whistling, and fell asleep again. The second time he awakened, Francis could hear nothing but his own breathing and the gentle sighing of the horses. There was no wind, no lashing snow. He stretched as much as the cramped space would allow, and felt Mr. Grimes move near him.

"Well, Mr. Tucket," the mountain man said, "should we see what it's like outside?"

Outside it was so white, so bright and dazzling that Francis had to close his eyes for a minute to keep from getting a headache. They had a bit of trouble getting out of their home—the snow had drifted nearly four feet deep over them—but once out, Francis was amazed to feel the warmth of the sun.

Mr. Grimes didn't allow him much time to marvel at things, or even over the fact that they were still alive.

"Come on, Mr. Tucket, we've got to put these horses back on their feet and get to Spot Johnnie's. We're not in clover yet . . ."

Getting the horses up turned out to be quite a job. They were stiff—Mr. Grimes said the only reason they hadn't frozen to death was that the snow had made a sort of blanket around them—and before they could stand, the circulation had to be rubbed back into their legs.

Once up, the mounts had to be walked back and forth through the snow to loosen them up some more. It was nearly an hour before Francis and Mr. Grimes loaded the beaver pelts and started off.

They had ridden hard—even in the storm—and Francis was surprised to find that they were much farther along than he had thought—well out of the main river valley they had tried to follow out of the canyon country and back up on the plains. It was a good thing, too. The deep snow in the bottom of the valley made it almost impossible to ride, and the horses floundered again and again.

Once they had fought their way to the top of the bluff wall—where the wind had swept the snow along—the going was much easier. There were drifts now and then, but they rode around the really big pileups.

It was cold—almost zero—but without the wind, and with the sun on his back, Francis felt fine. His mare was in good shape again, and the world was a bright new land—crisp, clean, alive. Steam boiled out of the ponies' nostrils.

They rode slowly most of the morning, letting the horses stop to graze now and then, and early in the afternoon, Mr. Grimes called a halt near a stand of brush.

"Why are we stopping so soon?" Francis asked. "We could make another ten miles before dark."

"And freeze to death, Mr. Tucket? They wouldn't find us until spring—if then. We're stopping to build a lean-to out of those willows and get a fire going. We're stopping to eat—if you can find some meat around here somewhere—*and* we're stopping to let this sun work on those beaver pelts for a spell. That take care of your question?"

Francis nodded, sliding from the mare. They cut the pelts loose and spread them, fur-side up to dry the moisture out of them. Then they tethered the horses, and Mr. Grimes took his knife and cut small willow poles for a shelter. Francis shouldered his rifle and ambled off in search of game.

They had been seeing rabbits all morning—jackrabbits in the open places, and cottontails in the brushy beds of streams. In only a few minutes he had got two of the bigger jackrabbits and was carrying them back to camp. There he found a cozy, three-sided bungalow waiting, with a roaring fire in front of it.

Mr. Grimes was standing near the fire, warming himself, and Francis smiled. It all looked like a picture his father had hung up in their barn back in Missouri. The picture showed an old lumberjack, in the middle of the woods, standing over a small fire warming his hands and grinning, while in the background, a bear was sneaking out of the lumberjack's tent with a side of bacon.

"You're sure grinning a lot, Mr. Tucket," the mountain man said with a snort. "Especially for someone who couldn't do any better than a couple of scruffy rabbits. I was sort of figuring on you bringing back an antelope or two . . ."

Francis told him about the picture in the barn, and Mr. Grimes snorted again.

"Must have been an eastern bear. Out here we've got grizzlies, at least up in the peaks. If a grizzly decided to take a side of bacon, he'd like as not take it over your body." While he talked, he was dressing out the rabbits and spitting them over the fire. Before long, they were sizzling and hissing.

They ate quietly—the rabbit meat so tough Francis thought his moccasins might be easier to chew—and after polishing off both rabbits, Mr. Grimes gathered up some of the pelts for the lean-to while Francis led the horses to a clear spot nearby so they could graze.

The afternoon turned to dark early, and with the darkness they heaped wood on the fire and went to sleep, wrapped in beaver pelts.

The next morning they were up before the sun. By first light—still stiff and a bit cold—they were riding. They rode at a good clip most of the day. By late afternoon, Francis could see smoke on the horizon, and he pointed it out to Mr. Grimes.

"I see it, Mr. Tucket. Spot Johnnie's, unless I miss my guess or took a wrong turn somewhere. Only . . ."

"Only what?"

"Only there seems to be a bit more smoke than

there should. Let's see if we can get a run out of these ponies."

He kicked Footloose in the ribs and upped his stride. Francis kneed his mare into a following gallop and the pack horses kept up.

There had been something different in the mountain man's voice—a hardness that wasn't usually there, not even when the Crows had jumped them. Francis wasn't sure, but he thought it was the first time he'd ever heard Mr. Grimes sound even a little alarmed.

And the smoke got thicker as they neared.

— Chapter Twenty-one —

ON THE RIDGE overlooking Spot Johnnie's Mr. Grimes pulled to a stop. Francis reined in beside him a second later. What met their eyes was total carnage.

Down below, *all* the buildings were on fire—including the storage sheds—and they were burning so fiercely that the snow around them was melted for more than a hundred feet.

Around the house area could be seen small humps, like gray rocks, scattered here and there. There were perhaps twenty of these humps, and with sudden shock, Francis realized that they were bodies. They rode down toward the house.

"Pawnees," Mr. Grimes said, examining several bodies. "Braid and his boys."

Above the burning trading post, toward the east about two miles, they now saw a wagon train of twenty or more wagons. These were not arranged in a circle, but scattered this way and that, and two of the wagons were burning. They looked like small torches in the snow.

Mr. Grimes heeled Footloose and started at a walk toward the house. His rifle was balanced across his lap, and his back was slouched in a way Francis had never seen.

Francis followed. The pack horses automatically followed and slowly the procession approached the trading post.

There were bodies of Pawnee Indians everywhere. They lay as they had fallen, some running, some stretched out as though sleeping.

"I count twenty-three," Mr. Grimes said. His voice was hollow. "Old Spot put up one whale of a fight."

They dismounted and searched the ground around the post, but could not find the bodies of Spot or his family.

"Maybe they got away," Francis offered, "and made it over to the wagon train."

"No-ah, Mr. Tucket. That's a nice thought, but there are too many dead braves around here. They wouldn't have let Spot get away."

"But they aren't out here . . ." Francis's voice trailed off as his eyes went to the still-burning house. The fire was roaring now, as the pitch in the log walls started to burn.

"In—in there?" Francis asked, pointing to the flames. "Spot . . . ?"

Mr. Grimes gave a short nod. He stood for a moment, watching the fire, breathing deeply. Then he broke off and studied the dead Indians on the ground.

"What are you looking for?" Francis asked.

The mountain man didn't answer. Presently he finished his examination, looked off across the hills, and mounted.

"C'mon, Mr. Tucket, let's go talk to the farmers."

When they were a hundred yards from the wagon train, three men came out to meet them. Two of them held rifles at the ready; the other one —in the middle—a stocky man with red hair and a red face, did the talking.

Mr. Grimes dismounted again. "They hit you long ago?" he asked.

"Maybe an hour, maybe more. Fifteen or so came down on our wagons and another forty jumped the trading post."

"You lose many men?"

"Two. Thing is, they kept us hopping while they nailed the post. We couldn't get out to help . . ."

Mr. Grimes nodded. "They were after powder. Did—did anyone get out of the house?"

The stocky man shook his head. "At least, if they did, we didn't see 'em. Friends of yours?"

Mr. Grimes was quiet, staring at the snow-covered hills.

"I know how you feel," the man went on. "One of the two we lost was my brother . . ."

There was silence for a while. Francis realized that the stocky man was crying, but that his lips were moving back and forth in anger.

Mr. Grimes broke the silence. "Well, it appears that the time has come to do something about Braid." He turned to look at Francis. "Remember me telling you, Mr. Tucket, that if I ever did kill Braid, it wouldn't be because he had something I wanted. This is different, Mr. Tucket, very different."

He walked over to Footloose, removed the saddle, threw it on the ground, and mounted bareback. "What's your name?" he asked the stocky man.

"Groves. Ben Groves."

"Well, Mr. Groves, I'd take it kindly if you'd keep you eyes on Mr. Tucket, the boy here, for me."

"Now wait a minute—" Francis began.

"There's a fair chance I won't be coming back from this ride," Mr. Grimes went on, ignoring Francis. "Fact is, he's kinda headstrong, and if somebody doesn't watch him, he's likely to do just about anything. Understand me, Mr. Groves?"

The redheaded man nodded. He motioned to the other two men, and before Francis could move, they had grabbed him, pulled him from his horse, and were holding him fast.

"Hey!" he yelled. "Wait a minute! Mr. Grimes, you can't just go out there and jump a whole tribe of Pawnee." He tried to wiggle free but failed. "They'll—they'll kill you. That's dumb. You can't do that, Mr. Grimes. You can't be dumb. You wouldn't let *me* be dumb . . ."

"Now, now, Mr. Tucket. You're rattling on, and that won't do at all. Mr. Groves, if I don't come back by morning, my saddle, all those beaver pelts, and the ponies belong to the boy. I'd be happy if you'd make sure he gets them—not, of course, that anybody'd be foolish enough to try to take them away from him."

"No!" Francis yelled.

"Also," the mountain man continued, "would your train be going to Oregon?"

Mr. Groves nodded. "The Willamette Valley."

"The boy's got folks out there. You might take him with you—maybe make him work his way."

"No! No!"

"I'll do everything you ask," the farmer answered. "I'll hand deliver him, with his pelts, to his folks if you want. But I'd rather be riding out with you . . ."

"No-ah, Mr. Groves. It just takes one. Two, and they'd kill us both. One, and I might get close enough—by insulting Braid."

"No!" Francis screamed again. "Even if you win, you lose. For what? There's no reason to die. It's done, Mr. Grimes—and done is done."

"And now, Mr. Tucket." The mountain man turned at last to Francis. "Before I go—and I don't want you getting some kind of swelled head out of this—I'd like to say it's been sort of fun having you around. Be seeing you . . ."

He wheeled his horse and started off, northeast, riding loose and fast.

"Mr. Grimes, come back!" Francis yelled after him. "Come back, come back, come back . . ."

But Footloose, without the saddle, gained speed rapidly and before Francis could think the mountain man had vanished in the dying evening light.

— Chapter Twenty-two —

FRANCIS RODE HARD.

It was a strange mount, but he now knew how to ride well enough to stay on almost any horse. This one was a big black—long legged and fresh. And stolen.

An hour after Mr. Grimes had gone, just after moonrise, Mr. Groves had made the mistake of not watching Francis closely. In a flash, he had run to the corral, thrown a war bridle on the black, and with nothing but his rifle, had left the camp.

The trail cut in the snow and lighted by the half

moon was easy to follow. But the hour lead Mr. Grimes had on him worried Francis. Footloose had been tired, it was true, but without a saddle—and considering also that Footloose was a big horse—it was entirely possible that Mr. Grimes would catch up to the Pawnees before Francis could catch up to him.

Francis drove the horse hard. Every time the black even thought of slowing, he laid his rifle barrel with a vengeance across the gelding's rump. What, exactly, he was going to do when and if he caught up with the mountain man, Francis wasn't sure. Try to stop him, of course, but—if he couldn't talk Mr. Grimes out of tangling with Braid, then at least help him. Two guns were always better than one.

Two hours of riding brought the moon higher and made it practically as light as day when it was actually almost ten o'clock at night.

Ten o'clock, Francis thought, goading the black to even longer strides. How I've changed. There was a time when ten o'clock at night meant getting wrapped in a huge quilt and bundled into bed, and feeling the warmth leave my face as the fire in the wood stove died. Died. There was a time when I didn't even think of things that died. I didn't know anything about all this killing. Nothing died, ever, except a farm animal now and then.

He pushed these thoughts from his mind. They were making him afraid—afraid that he might not catch up.

There would be times, later, when he would wonder about all the little things that kept him from reaching Mr. Grimes in time. If he had beat the black harder, or tried to make his break from the wagon train earlier . . .

As it was, he was only a split second late—the time that it takes a man to pull a trigger. He rode over a rise, and there, in a small, flat meadow, were Braid and Mr. Grimes.

They were riding hard at each other and, in the moonlight, the snow flying up around their horses as they closed looked like the fine spray thrown up in front of a ship. They were both stripped to the waist and carrying rifles. When the horses were fifty feet apart, the two men fired. Francis saw the rifles flash and both men tumble from their horse.

They had fired at the same instant, and the one-armed and one-braided men landed within ten feet of each other.

Francis's mind went blank when the mountain man fell from his horse. He rode up, dismounted, and if he noticed the fifteen mounted warriors on the other side of the battlefield, he gave no sign of it. He didn't care.

"Howdy, Mr. Tucket," the mountain man said, wincing as he pulled himself to a sitting position. His shoulder was turning red. "I sort of figured you'd be along. Glad you could make it in time for the fun . . ." He winced again.

Francis tore his shirt off and wrapped it around the shoulder. Mr. Grimes pushed him away. "No-ah, Mr. Tucket. Not done yet." He propped himself on one knee, then slowly stood, grunting, weaving.

"What do you mean?" Francis asked. "Braid's dead." He pointed to where the Indian lay in the snow. The mounted warriors were now around the body in a half circle. "It's done."

"Not done yet," Mr. Grimes repeated, stagger-ing. He pulled out his skinning knife. "One more thing to do." Weaving drunkenly, he made his way to the body of his enemy. Then he leaned down.

"No!" Francis screamed. "You *can't* . . ." He ran and pulled the mountain man away. This, some-how, was worse than all the rest. To kill Braid was one thing, perhaps even right, in the cold-blooded justice that ruled the prairie. But not this—this ani-mal thing.

"*Can't*, Mr. Tucket?" Mr. Grimes said, laughing

hoarsely. "And why not? He would have done the same to me . . ."

Francis stared in horror, then turned away. Many things were suddenly clear to him, and the biggest was that Mr. Grimes was right. He *could* do what he was doing, simply because he was ruled by the same law that ruled Braid. He was of the prairie, the land, the mountains—and was, in a way, a kind of animal. It was not wrong—not for Jason Grimes.

But for Francis Alphonse Tucket? For someone from a farm in Missouri? For someone with a family waiting in Oregon?

There were different rules for different people. One set for Mr. Grimes, but, Francis thought, as he reached his horse, there was a different set for him. He was *not* and did not want to be a "mountain man."

He mounted the horse. Mr. Grimes would be all right, he knew. The fight had been fair in the Indians' eyes, and besides, they wanted to keep on trading for powder. No, the Indians wouldn't kill Mr. Grimes, and his shoulder would heal. Soon he would be trapping again.

But this time without me, Francis told himself, squaring his shoulders. He wiped his eyes with the back of his hand. A boy named Francis Alphonse Tucket might stay and live wild and follow the beaver ponds. But Francis Alphonse Tucket wasn't a boy anymore. Jason Grimes had made that boy *Mr.* Tucket and Mr. Tucket was going to Oregon, to his family, to his kind of life—to his set of rules.

Francis slapped the horse as hard as he could and headed for the wagon train. And somehow he knew he'd better not look back at Mr. Grimes—not even to wave a good-bye.

GARY PAULSEN'S WESTERN SAGA
CONTINUES IN . . .

CALL ME FRANCIS TUCKET

After a year with Mr. Grimes, Francis has learned to live by the
harsh code of the wilderness. He can cause a stampede, survive
his own mistakes, and face up to desperadoes. But when he res-
cues a little girl and her younger brother, Francis takes on more
than he bargained for.

Available from Yearling Books

Excerpt from Call Me Francis Tucket *by Gary Paulsen*

Copyright © 1995 by Gary Paulsen

Published by Yearling
an imprint of
Random House Children's Books
a division of Random House, Inc.
New York

— Chapter Three —

"Ahh, see here, Dubs, what fate has provided for us . . . ," a deep, professorial-sounding voice boomed.

It was a dream, Francis was sure of it. It simply wasn't possible that a human voice could be speaking and for a full five seconds he refused to open his eyes and lose the relaxing comfort of sleep.

"Come now, lad. Don't be lazy. We have business afoot. Wake up."

Francis opened his eyes.

At first it didn't matter. The sun was full up and when his lids opened the brightness blinded him.

He blinked, let his eyes adjust, turned away from the sun and opened them again.

He was staring at the dead fire, or more accurately across the fire. There was a man sitting, squatting back on his haunches. He looked old to Francis, over forty, and was so heavily bearded Francis could not see his face for the hair.

But the clothing was more startling. The man was short, almost fat, and dressed in a black suit including a black vest, black boots, black trousers and black frock coat, and a full top hat on his head.

"See, Dubs, the lad awakens." The man smiled—his teeth broken and jagged; a bit of tobacco juice oozed out the side of the lip into the beard and the lines around his black eyes did not match the smile.

Francis slid his hand toward the rifle. Or where the rifle had been. He could not find it.

"See, Dubs, even now he reaches for his weapon. A true child of the frontier." The man spoke to somebody else—Francis couldn't see anybody at first—but kept looking at Francis. The smile widened. Like a snake getting ready to hiss. A hair snake. "I have your rifle—and a nice piece it is, too."

"What . . . who are you?" Francis at last found words. "What are you doing here?"

"Exactly!" The man nodded, waved a filthy finger. "That's exactly what *I* said, wasn't it, Dubs—when we came upon the lad, didn't I say just that? We came over the hill at dawn and I saw you sleeping there and saw your horse and I turned to Dubs and whispered—so as not to disturb your slumbers—and I said: Who is this, and what is he doing here?"

Francis sat up, or tried to. Something heavy, like warm iron, descended on his head and shoulders and pressed him back down. He swiveled his head back and saw that he was looking at a giant—a true giant. It was a man in crude buckskins, so large he seemed to blot out the sun, and Francis saw that the giant had put a hand down to keep him on the blanket.

"Dubs," the man across the fire said by way of introduction. "Isn't he something? There are some who have questioned his humanity, thinking he was of another species—men, I should hasten to add, who are not with us any longer, Dubs having sent them to the nether regions—but I do not question him. I am grateful that he is my partner, my right hand. He is Dubs. I am Courtweiler, although most call me simply Court. And you?"

Francis stared at him. Part of his mind was still trying to awaken and part of him was trying to accept that apparently these men meant to harm him. If they had been friendly they would not have taken his rifle. He realized that what had bothered him last night was his acting like an amateur, a greenhorn. He should have placed his bedroll well away from the fire, hidden so he would have time to react if enemies came. Stupid. Well, nothing for it now. He had to buy time, time to think, time to come up with a plan. "Francis," he said. "My name is Francis."

"Ahh—a proper name, that. Francis. I would have liked to have been named Francis but my ancestors came into it and I had to take the family name. Courtweiler isn't bad, but Francis—now that's a name, isn't it, Dubs?"

Francis looked up again and if the giant was listening at all he gave no indication. He held Francis down with one hand while staring out across the prairie.

"It was a stroke of good fortune coming upon you this way," Courtweiler added. "For us, that is. Not so good for you."

"What do you mean?" Francis looked at his rifle, which was across the fire on the ground leaning against Courtweiler's leg while he squatted. He couldn't reach it. And his possibles bag and knife were somewhere in back of him—he'd never get to them before Dubs landed on him.

"I mean, Francis, that we have a specific need for just about everything you have. Our equipment has run into the ground and we aren't halfway to that golden coast we aspire to. I'm afraid we're going to have to relieve you of your belongings."

"My belongings?"

Courtweiler nodded. "Exactly. Gun, horse, saddle—essentially everything. I think I could even fit into that buckskin shirt."

"My clothes, too?"

"Except your pants. I think we'll leave those in the interests of propriety. But everything else. And I don't want you to think I'm ungrateful. Indeed, if you will turn and look," he made a sign to Dubs, who stepped back and let Francis rise, "you will see that I am in desperate straits indeed. Even my mule suffers."

Francis rose to his knees and looked to the rear where an old mule, so skinny its ribs stuck out inches, stood with its head hanging nearly to the ground. On its back was a blanket worn until there were holes through it, no saddle, and instead of a bridle a loop went around the lower jaw. The miracle, Francis thought, was that the mule had gotten this far.

"You see what I mean." Courtweiler pointed to the mule. "Dubs prefers to go afoot, and by the third day will outrun a horse. But given as I am to more intellectual pursuits and less of the physical I need to ride. And so we must have your horse."

"I have kin," Francis said. "Just over that rise. They'll be looking for me . . ."

Courtweiler shook his head. "Dissembling won't help, my boy. We came from there. There are no people there, no tracks, nothing. I do not know how you arrived here but let me assure you, there is nobody close to help you."

"I'll die if you leave me here with nothing."

Courtweiler sighed. "Indeed. There is that possibility. Still, life on the frontier is very hard and we must expect these little setbacks and somehow muddle on, don't you agree? Now, please take off that shirt before I have to ask Dubs to assist you . . ."

Francis hesitated, saw Dubs move and decided not to anger the huge man. He shrugged out of his shirt, felt the morning coolness on his skin.

"Off the blanket, please."

Francis moved from the blanket and Dubs

snaked it off the ground and rolled it up in one fluid motion and stood again, still, waiting.

"And now, Francis, as fruitful as it has been to meet you, I'm afraid we must be off . . ."

Dubs had already caught the mare—Francis could not believe they had done all this without awakening him—and they saddled her, left the mule standing and rode off, Courtweiler holding Francis's rifle across his lap as they rode away, headed west while Francis sat next to a dead buffalo, a nearly dead mule, and watched them go.

**TURN THE PAGE FOR A PEEK AT ANOTHER
RIP-ROARING TUCKET ADVENTURE. . . .**

TUCKET'S RIDE

Join Francis Tucket and his adopted family, Lottie and
Billy, as they become entangled in the Mexican-American
War of 1848.

Available from Yearling Books

Excerpt from Tucket's Ride *by Gary Paulsen*

Copyright © 1997 by Gary Paulsen

Published by Yearling
an imprint of Random House Children's Books
a division of Random House, Inc.
New York

—— Chapter One ——

Francis Tucket lay on the ridge and watched the adobe hut a hundred yards away and slightly below him. He had his rifle resting on a hump of dirt, the sights unmoving, pointed at the doorway to the hut.

"Are we going to stay here forever? I mean it's really cold. I've been cold before but not like this." A small girl and boy stood ten yards to his rear with the horse and mule, all hidden below the level of the ridge. "It just seems that since you haven't seen anything, we could go down there and get warm. There might be a stove . . ."

"Please be quiet, Lottie." Francis turned and held his hand out. "Now. We're going to wait. I heard something somewhere down there that sounded like a scream. We're going to wait and watch. Be quiet."

There was a horse in front of the hut, tied to a half-broken hitch rail. Some chickens walked around the sides pecking at the dirt. There was no dog. Three goats were tied to stakes in back of the house. The horse had a familiar saddle on its back—military cut with the bedroll in front. The horse didn't look wet, so it hadn't worked hard getting here. Then, too, Lottie was right—it was cold, so the horse wouldn't show much sweat.

All this went into Francis's eyes and registered in his thoughts automatically—along with the direction of the wind, the fact that a coyote was off to the side a couple of hundred yards away eyeing the chickens, and a hawk was circling over the yard doing the same thing. All of it in and filed away.

There. A scream—short but high. Not a man. Maybe a child or a woman.

Well. That was all Francis thought: *Well*. If it was somebody needing help, he was in a bad place to give it. One fifteen-year-old boy, a young girl and a boy with him, a horse and a mule and one rifle.

Still. He couldn't stay and not help.

It's what he got for not going west, he thought—for not taking the two children and just heading out along the Oregon Trail to find his parents and the wagon train he had been kidnapped from almost two years ago. He and the children had made a good start west, then had gotten sidetracked as they crossed the prairie, and before he knew it an early fall had caught them short of the mountains. Snow had filled all the passes.

Somebody at a trading post on the trail had said that there was a southern route down in Mexico that stayed open all year, so Francis had started south. They couldn't hope to winter in the northern prairies. He hadn't realized that taking on Lottie and her little brother, Billy, would slow him down so. He had found them, alone on the prairie, after their father had died of cholera.

It had grown warmer as they had moved south along the mountains. Still cold at night, but they had picked up some wool blankets at the trading post, and Lottie had sewn pullover coats for all of them as they moved down into the territory belonging to Mexico.

There. He heard a thump, then a scream.

"You two stay here," he called softly to Lottie. "And I mean *stay* here. I'll be back."

He slid to the left where there was a thin brush line and followed it down to the hut. The building did not have a window, which was good, because the brush line was sparse scrub oak and the goats had long before stripped away the leaves.

Now Francis was barely concealed, and ran quickly, trying to keep his moccasins quiet.

He held himself still at the side of the hut, listening. Again, a muffled sound. He checked the cap on his rifle, cocked it, and moved to the side of the door.

He was five feet from the door when he noted that the saddle on the horse had a large us stamped on the sides, and the horse had the same brand on its shoulder. It was a United States Cavalry mount. Half a question formed in his mind—what was a United States Cavalry mount doing in Mexican territory?—when the door blew open and a young woman ran out, a large man behind her. He grabbed her shoulders.

"Get back in here!"

Half a second: Her eyes were wide with terror; she had a scuff on her face where she'd been hit. The man's blue uniform shirt was ripped. He had a bloody scratch on his cheek. He was wearing a military belt with a flap-covered holster, and he saw Francis, threw the woman aside, and clawed at the holster.

"Wait . . . ," Francis got out, then saw the flap of the holster come up, the hand catch the butt of the revolver, the barrel swing toward him as the man cocked it, an explosion of smoke and noise.

Francis felt the ball cut his cheek and burn past and he shot from the hip. His rifle recoiled in his hands and he saw the ball strike the man high in the chest. He saw everything: a little puff of dust from the blue shirt as the ball hit; no blood, but dust, and then the man went backward and down to a sitting position. He looked up at Francis and said, "You've killed me," and settled on his back slowly and died.

All in three seconds. Francis stood in silent horror. He felt the sun on his back, the terrified woman standing in front of him, the goats bleating nearby, the smoke from the shots drifting off to the side. He stood there and knew that nothing would ever be the same again.

He had killed a man.

DON'T MISS ANY OF THE BOOKS IN THE TUCKET ADVENTURES!

Share the excitement of Francis Tucket's travels as he heads west on the Oregon Trail.

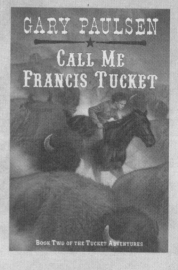

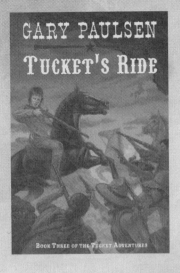

GARY PAULSEN
TUCKET'S RIDE

BOOK THREE OF THE TUCKET ADVENTURES

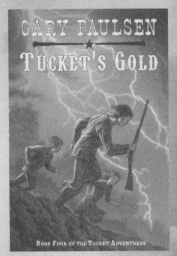

GARY PAULSEN
TUCKET'S GOLD

BOOK FOUR OF THE TUCKET ADVENTURES

GARY PAULSEN
TUCKET'S HOME

BOOK FIVE OF THE TUCKET ADVENTURES